Candy Sky Tells A Lie

Shanna P. Lowe

CANDY SKY TELLS A LIE

This book is a work of fiction. Names, characters, businesses, organizations, places, events, and incidents are either the products of the Author's imagination or used fictitiously. Any resemblance to actual persons, living or dead, or locales is entirely coincidental.

To request permissions, contact the publisher at shanna@shannaplowe.com.

www.shannaplowe.com

Edited by Tally Ink
Cover Art by Angelique Modin
Layout & Interior Illustrations by LeighAnn Sutton

First Edition: September 2022

Hardback ISBN: 979-8-9859564-1-2
Paperback ISBN: 979-8-9859564-0-5
eBook ISBN: 979-8-9859564-2-9

LCCN: 2022905642

For Maddie

Candy Sky Tells A Lie

Contents

New Message

To : <Samantha Sky>

Subject : Candice Sky

To the Parents or Guardians of Candice Sky,

I am writing to you out of concern for your daughter's missing project due last Monday. She claims that a pipe in the bathroom broke, flooding the apartment and soiling her project. If you could confirm her story, I would be happy to give Candice extra time on this project.

Candice is such a joy to have in class.
I look forward to her success!

Sincerely,
Mrs. Gulligan
7th & 8th Grade
English Teacher

New Message

To : <Samantha Sky>

Subject : Candice Sky

To the Parents or Guardians of Candice Sky,

I am writing to you out of concern for your daughter's study guide for an upcoming test. She insisted that it, and I quote, "had a bath in the fryer and was served to a customer" at a local fast food restaurant. I struggle to understand her story, so if you could contact me for clarification, that would be appreciated. Thank you!

Candice is such a joy to have in class.
I look forward to her success!

Sincerely,
Mrs. Gulligan
7th & 8th Grade
English Teacher

New Message

To : <Samantha Sky>

Subject : Candice Sky

To the Parents or Guardians of Candice Sky,

I am writing to you out of concern for your daughter's failed test. Her latest anecdote has her stranded on a boat after hitting an iceberg that destroyed the motor. Because she had to wait most of the night for a rescue boat, she was too exhausted to focus on the exam. Forgive me for saying I find the story a bit unbelievable. Please contact me at your earliest convenience.

Candice is such a joy in class.
I look forward to her success!

Sincerely,
Mrs. Gulligan
7th & 8th Grade
English Teacher

Send

New Message

To : <Samantha Sky>

Subject : Candice Sky

To the Parents or Guardians of Candice Sky,

I have yet to hear from you regarding your daughter's missing assignments and grades. Perhaps email is not the best mode of communication. I will be calling to set up a parent-teacher conference. Let me know what time works best for you.

Thank you.

Sincerely,
Mrs. Gulligan
7th & 8th Grade
English Teacher

ONE
My Little Secret

Neiwood School District
Neiwood, CA
Missed Calls (2)

Mom's phone rings again. I jab the red end-call button and swallow. Air grinds down my throat like bare skin on a dry tube slide. Why does Mrs. Gulligan have to be so persistent?

I listen for the running shower from the only bathroom in our apartment, praying Mom takes her time under the hot spray. My foot ricochets against the hardwood floor of the den with nervous energy. I can't even concentrate on my favorite show, *Young, Bold, and Beautiful,* as it plays on the wall-mounted television. It trails several tween fashion designers sewing and piecing together outfits for models. It's the premiere of the newest season, something I've been counting down to for months. Now, I'd have to watch the recording later.

Thanks, Mrs. Gulligan.

This is all because of that ridiculous essay due yesterday. The one focusing on a book I may or may not have read. I can't help it, though! I have seven classes to manage. Seven. No one should put that kind of pressure on a thirteen-year-old.

I press my finger against the touchpad and watch the screen unlock. Mom doesn't know I saved my fingerprint on her phone. As I open her email app, I remember the test I flunked last week. Twenty-five multiple choice questions followed by three essay questions. Anyone who can finish that in fifty minutes isn't human.

There are also a few assignments that slipped my mind earlier this month. And the other essay from a while back. Again, *seven* classes. Mrs. Gulligan can't blame me.

I open a blank email and type:

Dear Mrs. Gulligan

What would Mom say to my English teacher? I chuckle uneasily. I'd be dead if she actually knew about my grades. Not really. She would probably ship me off to Grandma Carrie for fall break, grounded inside her house of creepy antique dolls and an ungodly amount of shrieking parrots. Mom has done it before. I still have nightmares from decades of dust and feathers—dead, glassy eyes following my every movement.

I glance at the bathroom door on the corner of the hallway that leads to our bedrooms. Steam rises out from the crack at the bottom and wafts through the den, making the air hot and uncomfortably humid. Good. Keep showering, Mom.

Dear Mrs. Gulligan,

Sorry to have missed your calls. I am a flight

attendant and spend most of my time on an airplane.

That's sort of the truth. Mom does occasionally work as a flight attendant when someone calls out sick or has a family emergency. Usually, she's a reserve, checking people in at the gate while on standby. She goes on, maybe, four or five flights a year.

Contacting me by phone will not work due to my busy schedule and constant change in time zones. Please continue to email.

Emails are easy to delete. Phone calls? Not so much. They're dangerous.

As for your concerns regarding my daughter Candy, I can safely vouch for every incident she has claimed. She has such bad luck.

Bad luck when it comes to English teachers. Why can't Mrs. Gulligan leave me alone like the others? They hardly bat an eye when I miss an assignment, opting for communication through the online parent portal (which *mysteriously* had a glitch that changed the password at the beginning of the school year).

Perhaps her persistence could have something to do with the rumors circulating about her.

My best friend Maggie swears on her life that Mrs. Gulligan is a witch. A living, breathing, cauldron-stirring, broom-riding, frog-eating witch.

Maggie claims that Mrs. Gulligan cursed a boy named Sayer Lafayette after he was caught paying classmates to write his papers. Every dollar bill he touched turned into dried leaves. Coins became acorn caps. If that wasn't enough, his perfectly smooth angel face grew massive boils that oozed greenish white pus. No one could look at him without gagging.

Do I believe Maggie? Absolutely not.

If she were a witch, Mrs. Gulligan would have found a way to contact my parents.

Please grant Candy extra time for these assignments. I'll make sure she gets them done by the end of September.

Sincerely,
Samantha Sky

My thumb hovers over the send button. I re-read the email, double-checking for errors and clarity. I certainly sound like my mother. Prim and proper. Practically her middle name.

A wormy sliver of doubt wriggles in my mind, softening my earlier determination. This email will officially open a line of communication between Mom and Mrs. Gulligan. Bile rises at the realization. "Mom" must admit to reading the other emails.

I picture the email tennis match I'll have to play in that scenario.

By not replying, Mrs. Gulligan might actually give up. Eventually. Hopefully.

With a sigh, I tap the trash icon. I have to prevent Mom from answering Mrs. Gulligan's calls somehow. There's more at stake than a summer with Grandma Carrie.

The Fall Equinox Dance.

When fliers for the dance appeared around school, I secretly ripped one from a bulletin board and taped it to my bathroom mirror. I read the flier every morning, planning what will be the greatest moment of my life.

Unlike other middle school dances where the dress code calls for jeans and t-shirts, the

Fall Equinox Dance mimics a high school prom. Only eighth graders are allowed to attend. We get to wear dresses and heels and make-up and doll our hair up with spray and shimmer and–

I exhale noisily, a tornado of fantasies leaving me winded. I've seen these dances all the time in movies, but to actually experience one? The idea leaves goosebumps on my skin. It's not just because it's a day dedicated to glamor and DJ tunes. I'll fulfill a lifelong dream of mine.

Perhaps not lifelong. But I have daydreamed about it since starting middle school.

The dream?

A boyfriend.

And not just any boyfriend.

Elijah Nole.

The rising pop singer who happens to be in the same grade at my middle school.

I met Elijah in-person on the second day of sixth grade. Or rather, his soccer ball met my face during PE, knocking me clear off my feet. Dazed and bleeding from my nose, I barely recognized Elijah helping me up and dusting me off until I was inches away from his warm amber eyes and worried frown. His voice, asking me if I was okay, was as calming as rain pattering against leaves. His touch a comfortable sea breeze. His presence was like taking a bite of the world's finest chocolate, hazelnut-ganache center and all. I wanted more.

My dream is for Elijah to sweep me off my feet and, quite possibly, share a first kiss with. To rest a hand on my hip on the dance floor, lean me backwards, gaze into my eyes, and whisper, "Candy Sky, you're the only girl for me."

Blood rushes to my cheeks. I squeal and hide my face in my hands.

"What are you doing on my phone?"

I jolt. The phone slips from my fingers and clatters face down on the floor. I scramble for it, chest heaving. I check for damages (and if I actually deleted that email). The screen is black except for the time and lock icon. I can't use my fingerprint with Mom watching me from the bathroom door.

Her arms cross over her plush robe. A towel twists on the top of her head, drying her brown hair.

When did the water turn off?

"Seriously, what are you doing?" She plods over and holds out her hand.

"N-Nothing!" I almost pull the phone away from her but doing so indicates guilt.

I give her the phone shakily.

She presses her thumb against the lock pad. Her eyes narrow on the screen. "You were obviously doing something on my phone."

"You left it on and—" *Think, Candy. Think.* "—I needed to look up information for an assignment. I couldn't use my phone since you took it away."

"Why is the email app open?" she asks.

I shrug and lean back on the couch nonchalantly. The trick is to look relaxed. Don't break eye contact. Twirl a strand of hair. Appear annoyed that someone doesn't believe you.

"It must have opened when I dropped the phone," I say. "Seriously, I was on the school's website looking up an assignment."

She purses her lips together, unconvinced. There's no evidence of any wrongdoing. Innocent until proven guilty, right? Eventually, she lets it slide. Mom crosses the den to her Bluetooth speaker and presses play.

I relax as soft jazz floats through the room. Silly coffee quotations on colorful canvases hang from the walls. Home Is Where the Coffee Pot Is. Live Life to the Fullest Cup. My Coffee Needs Coffee. Throw pillows on the cream-color furniture feature cappuccinos so realistic that I'm pretty sure you can taste the espresso. And the smell of coffee clings to everything in this apartment. Mom is addicted.

Mom's shift at the airport starts in an hour, so she heads down a short hallway to her bedroom and disappears inside. She shuts the door behind her.

On the rare occurrence that I venture inside, I'm met with clothes vacuumed in airlock bags and the smell of organic all-purpose cleaner mixed with, of course, coffee. Mom's room is never out of place.

Mine on the other hand . . . I like to tell Mom tiny elves have dress-up parties. They cover every surface with my clothes and play 52-Card Pickup with my schoolwork. Not only do they never win the game, but they also leave their garbage and dirty plates all over.

Curse those pesky elves!

I sprawl on the couch, lift the remote, and increase the volume. I watch the montage of tweens fitting their outfits onto their live models. The theme is a cocktail party. They have to create dresses worthy of high-end social and business networking.

I'd give anything to be one of those models, dripping in beautiful designer clothes and accessories. Elijah would definitely notice me then. I wonder if there's a way I can apply to the show.

Through the wall, Mom's phone blares Mozart's symphony, and my heart sinks.

Could it be Mrs. Gulligan?

"Don't answer!" I spring off the couch, run down the short hallway, and pound on her bedroom door. "It's spam callers! Dangerous spam callers!"

When Mom doesn't answer, I back up a few feet and crouch into my best impersonation of a football player. I shout a battle cry and barrel forward, tensing my shoulder for impact.

The door opens.

I yelp, momentum too strong to stop, and I collide with Mom. We fall into a pile of groans and tangled limbs. I wince as her elbow juts into my ribs.

"Hello?" a disgruntled voice says from beside us. "Samantha, are you there?'

Her phone!

I kick and squirm my way free, and then snatch it up.

"We don't want your overpriced vacuum, you scheming salesman!" I cry. "Now stop calling this number before I report you to the police!"

"Candice?" the person on the other side says.

That's not Mrs. Gulligan.

"Aunt Becky?"

"No, it's a scheming salesman," she snorts sarcastically.

Oops.

I open my mouth to respond, but the phone is yanked out of my hand. Soon, I'm on the receiving end of Mom's infamous you-are-so-dead glares.

"Candice Lynn Sky!" she says. "What on earth has gotten into you!"

"I-I thought . . ." I stutter, tailing off as embarrassment paints my cheeks bright pink.

"How would you know it's spam callers? And how did you get past the lock screen in the first place?"

Aunt Becky calls our names, but Mom ignores her. She taps and swipes her screen, eyes flickering back and forth swiftly. What is she reading? I bite my lip and fidget my thumbs.

Please let that email be deleted.

Please don't let Mom see the school district's calls.

Mom huffs before pressing the phone back to her ear. She frowns suspiciously at me but turns away. My shoulders sag. Luck is on my side. This time.

"You're asking me what that was about?" Mom barks an incredulous laugh. "Who knows! I can already feel my hip bruising." She massages the spot, wincing.

I frown. I didn't mean to cause an injury.

I want to apologize, but Mom ushers me out before I utter the words. The door slams in my face. The lock clicks.

For a moment, I stand completely still and breathe. That was much too close for comfort. I need to be more cautious next time.

I force myself back to the couch. Energetic techno plays from the TV as models strut down the runway. It's the judgment portion of the show, which will be followed by the elimination of one unfortunate tween. Whoever wins the entire season gets $10,000 and a scholarship to Sarian Design Academy.

Usually, I sit on the edge of my seat, hands clasped together, and maniacally mutter to myself who deserves to move onto the next round and who should be sent home. Right now, though, all I can focus on is my queasy stomach.

Part of me knows it's only a matter of time before my gig is up. Although eighth grade started a month and a half ago, I'm already not doing so hot in my classes. My parents will inevitably learn of my poor grades during parent-teacher conferences. But I'm okay with that. They are held in October. The dance is at the end of September. By the time my parents do find out, I'll have completed my lifelong goal and can write letters to Elijah from Grandma Carrie's house.

Once I make Elijah my boyfriend, of course.

I just have to make sure Mom and Dad don't find out my secret before the Fall Equinox Dance.

TWO
Lying is Like Fishing

I dip my paddle into the water and gently propel my inflatable board over the deeper parts of Morgan Bay. I sit with my legs submerged over the sides. The bottom half of my wetsuit is soaked, but I'm warm and snug. I don't dare stand, though, not like Maggie who balances perfectly on her inflatable paddle board next to me. A mesh satchel drapes her shoulder, bulging with waterlogged cans and other garbage.

The tune of Elijah Nole's hit single "We Stop for No One" drifts from the beach, too far away for me to hear the words, but I know the song by heart and sing the lyrics under my breath. On shore, the music blasts from a local radio station firing t-shirts from cannons at random passersby. Food trucks park in the sand with hordes of people swarming for cheese curds and freshly dipped corn dogs. The end-of-summer BBQ is as big as Christmas in Neiwood, and I've gone since before I can remember. Not only will the city host a bonfire tonight but also a firework show over the abandoned lighthouse.

Maggie spots a plastic bag floating nearby. She leans over, her dark brown side braid dipping into the water, and scoops up the bag with the blade of her paddle. She stores it in her mesh bag, tightening the drawstrings with a satisfied pull.

"Finally!" I say. "What time is it? I don't want to miss the raffle drawing."

"Calm down. We have twenty minutes." She pushes her wet braid over her shoulder and then checks her phone, which hangs from her neck in a protective silicon pouch.

I itch with jealousy. My phone has been confiscated and locked in a password-protected jail box. Courtesy of Mom. She caught me in the act of making fake vomit to get out of cleaning our bathroom. I guess I should have smushed the hotdogs before mixing them with overcooked oatmeal, not cut them into perfectly even slices. And I should have "vomited" into the toilet, not dramatically onto the kitchen floor.

"Do you know how many microplastic particles we're preventing by cleaning up the bay?" Maggie asks, coming up beside me. Sweat and saltwater beads on her arms and face, making her brownish yellow skin glow. "Not enough to make an impact on the overall health of the ocean, but at least our favorite beach will be cleaner. Did you know there are over—"

"Ninety-five thousand metric tons of microplastic particles in the ocean?" I finish for her with a smile. "See? I do pay attention to you."

"An astounding feat considering your brain only has room for Elijah Nole."

I slap water in her direction.

"Apparently, I have enough room for you, too, if I'm out here helping you earn clout with your new eco group."

With a mischievous glint in her eye, Maggie unzips her wetsuit to reveal a lime green shirt with a glittery pink font that reads "SASS: Save Aplysia Sea Slugs," above a cartoon-version of a brown slug.

"We are SASS! Hear us roar!" she shouts.

I duck my head and cover my face. Does she have no shame? "You're embarrassing me!"

When she's not sporting a wetsuit, Maggie wears shirts that read things like "Ditch Plastic and Save Lives" and "Fish Need Clean Water Too," so I shouldn't be surprised that she wore her eco group's uniform. But seriously, who wears clothes under their wetsuit?

"Oh, hush you. It's your obsession with Elijah Nole that's embarrassing." Maggie zips her wetsuit back up.

"I'm not obsessed."

"Sure you're not." Maggie purses her lips. "Last week I caught you reading fanfiction of him online."

"Did I do that?" I peer at an orange starfish below us, noting how it matches my earrings.

“And a couple days ago, you lied to someone that Elijah is your boyfriend and invited you to the dance.”

“I mean—” I roll my eyes “—it’s only a matter of time. He’ll be my boyfriend eventually. Is it really a lie if he’s going to ask me out, even if he doesn’t know it yet?”

“And yesterday—”

“Okay, okay!” I wave her off. "No need to list off everything."

“I’m just making sure you don’t turn into one of those creepy fangirl stalkers,” Maggie says. She submerges her hand into the water and wriggles her fingers. “It’s okay for you to have a crush on a celebrity. I have my fair share. But I think you’re taking this thing with Elijah Nole too far—no offense.”

“Yes, Mom,” I say, feeling a slight sting from my friend’s words. I’m not too surprised, though. Maggie has never exactly been into boys. At least, not in the way I am. Scuba camp and school are her top priorities, leaving her little time to dabble with a boyfriend.

That’s not to say she has never had one. In first grade, there was a boy she held hands with during recess for a couple of days. That’s a long time when you’re seven.

But she's yet to have one since starting middle school. Neither have I. Despite us being the two coolest people on the planet, we are practically invisible. Not popular enough to be noticed, and not unpopular enough to attract trouble. Finding a potential boyfriend, specifically Elijah Nole, is hard when you're the occasional seat cushion when someone doesn't see you already sitting in a chair.

Yes, I've been accidentally sat on. Twice.

"Can we please go enjoy ourselves like everyone else?" I eye a group of kids from our school.

I recognize the black stack of curls, dark skin, and red tracksuit of one boy, Sayer Lafayette, right away. He is the center of all the witch rumors regarding Mrs. Gulligan. I squint at his hands and notice his gloves. On the beach? I wonder if money actually turns to leaves and acorn caps with his touch.

I shake my head. Just the thought of Sayer Lafayette reminds me of the essay I forgot to write for Mrs. Gulligan. I don't want my mood soured, so I ignore him.

Another familiar face catches my attention, and I suck in a breath. The hairs on my arms rise. Excitement surges my body, and I lash out, gripping Maggie's ankle to ground myself, nearly causing her to fall off her board.

"Look over there!" I point to a girl our age talking with one of the DJs under the radio station's tent. "Laurell Mayflower Reynolds."

Her presence always reminds me of the drooping, feathery heads of a peony in an English garden. Delicate, beautiful, and sweet—peonies are the symbol of good fortune and riches. Laurell wears nothing but the latest designer collections. I wouldn't be surprised if her ruffly tank top, faded jeans, and crystal earrings cost over five hundred dollars. Her makeup looks professionally done, but those who follow her social media know she's a viral makeup artist. She's always setting new trends and making deals with boutique makeup companies.

Laurell is one of the most popular girls in Magnolia. Practically royalty.

What's even better?

Laurell is Elijah Nolc's cousin.

My eyes sweep the crowd for a glimpse of the rising pop singer. They are always, *always* together. Unfortunately, I don't see his freckled face or his trademark tie-dyed hoodie and neon shorts, so that must not be the case today.

Bummer. It's a little disappointing, but I can make the best of this situation.

Laurell being here puts me one step closer to making Elijah Nole my boyfriend.

"Let's go talk to her." I begin paddling toward the shore.

"You can't be serious!" Maggie tries to cut me off, but I dodge around her board. "Candice Lynn Sky!"

She sounds like my mother using my full name. I must have hit a nerve.

"What's the harm?" I ask, watching a speedboat zip by.

"Are you forgetting what she did last year?" Maggie drawls.

Somehow, I knew she would bring up *that incident*.

I brace myself, the waves of the boat spinning our boards away from one another. I rush to straighten, not wanting to lose sight of Elijah Nole's cousin for a second.

"No one confirmed Laurell was the person who switched Beth Abbot's face cream for hot sauce," I say, paddling back to Maggie.

"The video on her social feed of Beth screaming in the girls locker room says otherwise," Maggie snipes.

"It was a repost. Someone else must have pranked her."

She scoffs. "It wasn't a prank. It was bullying. Plain and simple."

"Look, all we're doing is talking to her for a bit." As well as asking her to hang out after school sometime, exchange numbers, and maybe introduce me to Elijah while she's at it. Easy-peasy lemon squeezy.

Maggie's cheeks fill with air before she exhales loudly. When her shoulders deflate, I know I won, and I mentally fist pump.

"What would we even talk about?" she asks.

"Something interesting," I grin. "Something that will keep the conversation going and make her, you know, want to hang out with us."

"Like what?"

"Hmmm." *Think, Candy, think.* "We'll tell her we're related to someone famous. That always works."

"No it does not!" Maggie digs her paddle into the water, coming to an abrupt stop. "I hate when you lie. You do it so often, and I can never keep up. Half the time I have to back you up. It's exhausting!"

Here we go with Ms. Never-Do-Anything-Bad. Seriously, a little lie here and there never hurts anyone. At least, not too seriously. In fact,

I think she would be pretty good at lying if she gave it a shot.

Lying is a lot like fishing. The bait and line and technique you use depends on the type of person you want to snare. Sometimes you get a bite, and sometimes you don't. The key is observation. Know which fish is more likely to nibble and which fish is more likely to notice your shadow. Someone like Maggie, who is a walking encyclopedia of everything marine and fishing related, could probably persuade the hardest of believers.

Of course, the day she takes up lying will be the day she trades in her fishing pole for cheerleader pom poms—never.

I still remember the pinky swear she insisted on when we became BFFs in kindergarten, after she learned of my totally awesome lying superpower: *We must never lie to each other. Doing so is against our friend code, the ultimate no-no*—her words, not mine. I think she wanted to make sure I treated her above everyone else, as BFFs do.

Shockingly, I have never broken our promise. Ever.

"Oh, Maggie. Sweet, sweet Maggie."

"Don't 'sweet Maggie' me!"

I look over my shoulder, at the distance building between us. "If you don't want to do this, I won't force you. But I need this."

I need Elijah Nole.

I continue gliding over the water.

"Candy, please think like a rational human being for one second!"

Too late.

I reach the shallow waters of the bay, just a few feet away from Laurell. I call out to her from my board, interrupting her conversation with the DJ. Laurell seems a little confused and looks over her shoulders to make sure that I'm not talking to someone else. I roll my eyes and beckon her over.

As she approaches, I gape at the sight of her blouse. The gold initials DSC are engraved under the left strap. I cannot believe she's wearing the latest designer clothes from the David Silk Collection. I would give anything to be her right now.

Act cool, I tell myself when I start to fluster.

"You go to Magnolia Middle School, right?" I initiate an icebreaker, resting my paddle on my lap.

Laurell furrows her eyebrows, perfectly shaded to match the newest trend. She nods with a guarded expression. "I'm in her science class." She points over me to Maggie who, in return, gives an awkward wave. "I don't think I know you, though."

"You should." I puff out my chest. "I'm Candy Sky, after all."

"Candy Sky." Laurell's nose crinkles in thought. "Where have I heard that name before?"

"Probably because I won state championships for the local swim team." I flick a lock of brown hair off my shoulder.

Out of the corner of my eye, Maggie's mouth drops open. I shift so she's out of my view. I don't want her ruining my mojo.

"That must be it," Laurell says. "Although, I could have sworn it was Brittany Pearl."

"Oh, uh . . . She won last year. I won this year."

"Are you sure? 'Cus I'm friends with–"

"Yes! I'm sure!" I say with more force than I intend.

Laurell's eyes narrow. I offer her a wide smile, thumbing my friendship bracelet. An octopus charm hangs from the gold chain. Maggie wears a matching one. We bought them for our one-year anniversary back in the first grade. The smooth metal, warmed by the heat of my skin, always provides comfort when I'm nervous or upset.

"Oh, Candice," Maggie singsongs. "I think it's time we go home."

I wave her off.

"I was wondering if I could ask you a few questions for my cousin. She's a TV show host down in Hollywood, and she wanted to know if I could help her interview some of my classmates," I say.

Her chortling "no way" and "which show" are music to my ears. Laurell claps her hands together and jumps up and down.

"The topic is middle school dating." I use my best reporter voice. "Are you comfortable answering a few questions?"

"Will I be on TV? Or flown to the show?" Laurell gushes.

"Maybe," I wink.

"What's your cousin's name? What talk show does she host?"

Details, Laurell wants details. Of course she does.

One trick I've learned is that, when coming up with details for a lie, it is best to use your surroundings. A guy in yellow swim trunks passes behind Laurell, and my ideas begin spinning. Yellow. Y. Think of a name that starts with Y.

"Her name is Yo . . ." I pause, thinking.

"Yo?" Laurell sounds disbelieving.

"Yolanda," I correct. "Yolanda Nox."

"What's her show called?"

"*The Yolanda Show.*" I relax my shoulders and swirl a finger around a lock of my hair.

"Oh my gosh, let me look it up." Laurell taps excitingly on her phone.

"No! You won't find anything!" I say, louder than I mean to.

Laurell startles. She looks at me like I've lost my mind, and I realize my paddle fell into the water during my panic. Laughing awkwardly, I quickly retrieve it.

"Her show is new—gonna air in a few weeks," I lie, cringing. "I'm not supposed to talk about it."

"That's strange," she frowns. "Wouldn't her marketing team want to hype up the show before it airs? Otherwise, no one will know about it."

"Uh, well, she's . . . still gathering materials and rehearsing."

"She hasn't started filming episodes?" Laurell asks. "Don't shows finish a season of episodes before release day?"

"Good question." I smile, eye twitching. "I'll have to ask her when she calls next."

"Maybe she's a morning talk show host," she says. "They host their shows live, versus late night hosts who film in advance."

I snap my fingers. "That's what she is! A morning talk show host."

"And you said her name is Yolanda Nox?" Laurell asks.

I nod.

Something hard hits the back of my board. I lose balance. The world tilts as I fall into the bay. Bubbles escape my parted mouth before I realize I'm fully submerged under water. I flail my arms and legs, desperate to find the surface. I've never been good at swimming.

My feet hit a pillow of sand on the bay's floor. That's right. We're in the shallows. Two feet at most. I stand up, break through the surface, and gasp.

Laurell pinches her lips together, hiding her snorts. Soon, her amusement becomes too much and she cackles raucously. Mortified, I whip my head toward Maggie. Soggy strings of brown hair smack my cheeks, bangs worming over my eyes. Her board scrapes against mine, and she holds the carry handle to prevent it from drifting away.

"Oops, my bad!" Maggie says innocently. "Lost control over my board. Good thing you're a state champion swimmer."

I glower at her, tempted to knock Maggie off her board. I can't believe her! My earlier confidence erodes with each droplet of water dribbling down my face. I climb back onto my board and force myself to smile at Laurell.

"I'll get back to you tomorrow at school." I turn around and paddle toward our garbage bags on shore, ignoring the disappointed call from Laurell about my cousin.

Maggie trails not far behind. I can tell by the sound of her paddle hitting the water and her shimmering reflection. She is standing again.

When we are far enough away from Laurell, I spin around. I try crashing the nose of my board into hers, but I miss by a few inches. Maggie is startled, nonetheless. She squawks and crouches down for balance.

"Why did you do that!" I demand. "Laurell probably thinks I'm a total loser now!"

Straightening, she tucks a loose strand of hair behind her ear. "I was saving you from yourself."

We glare at each other for a moment before Maggie's shoulders start to tremble. She covers her mouth and tries to stifle her giggles.

Eventually, though, Maggie bends over, grabs her belly, and guffaws.

"You? A state champion swimmer!" she gasps between laughs. "How did you come up with that?"

"Are you implying that it's impossible?" I ask, lifting my chin. Her laughter is infectious, and I feel a tremble in my chest. "I most certainly could be a champion swimmer, if I tried."

"You can't even run a mile for gym class." She wipes away a tear, trying to catch her breath.

"I'm not built for running."

"You're not built for swimming either," she says. "You look like a cat that's been thrown into water."

"Cats can swim! In fact, you'd be surprised. They're natural and powerful swimmers."

"Candy," she says in a voice that, once again, reminds me of my mother. "Serious talk, now. Listen up, okay? You gotta stop with the lying. It's becoming a real issue, and I'm worried about you. What happens when Laurell finds out your celebrity cousin doesn't exist? Someone is bound to catch you in a lie."

"No one ever does."

"They will, one day. What then?"

“You’re acting like a little white lie here and there is the end of the world,” I say before grinning. “If anything, I’m nurturing my creativity. Don’t think of it as lying, but as storytelling.”

“You’re impossible.” She clicks her tongue but doesn't argue any further.

One day, she’ll realize I’m right. And on that day, I’ll be walking arm in arm with Elijah Nole into the gymnasium full of colorful party lights and the live DJ vibrating the floor.

I can’t wait to tell Maggie I told you so.

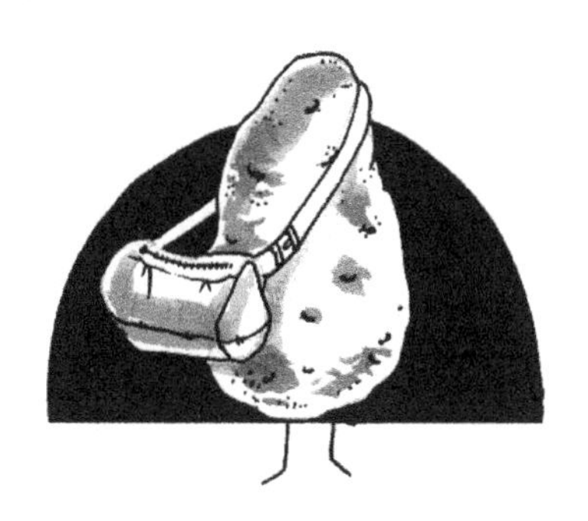

THREE
Hot Potato

As I walk up the waterlogged staircase leading to Mom's apartment, after Maggie's dad dropped me off from the beach BBQ, I wonder how I'm going to handle the Mrs. Gulligan situation. Sunday is almost over, and I doubt Mrs. Gulligan will appreciate me forgetting my homework, again. Maybe there's a way to bribe her, like I can with Mom and coffee. I know Mrs. Gulligan loves chocolate, always sneaking pieces into her mouth during class.

Thinking, I stare at the exterior paint shedding palm-sized flakes, ignoring the constant smell of burnt asparagus that lingered over Sandypoint Apartments. I stop at a Pepto-Bismol door with a chalk-paint sign hanging below the peephole. Live, Laugh, Love, & Lattes. Mom's touch.

I jab my key into the lock and open the door. I kick off my flip-flops, spraying sand everywhere, and head to the bathroom to wash my grimy hands. Dried seaweed sticks to my forehead, and I reek of sea brine.

While fixing my ponytail in the mirror, I hear a yowl at my feet and look down. Pickles, the world's fattest cat, is a black and white bowling ball with pudgy paws and a feather duster for a tail. He rubs his fluffy cheek against my ankle before opening his mouth, revealing his pink and black tongue, and chomping down. Hard.

"Ouch!" I yank my foot away.

He goes after the other one.

I cry as his teeth sink into my flesh. It's not enough to break the skin, but it hurts like nobody's business.

"You stupid cat! Alright, alright! I'll give you food."

I dodge his bites on the way to the kitchen and grab a can of wet food from the cupboard underneath Mom's three-hundred-dollar espresso machine. The chrome appliance takes up most of the counter space, and there are a number of times I've walked in on Mom praying to the glorified thing.

"You aren't feeding him, are you?" Mom materializes out of nowhere.

I screech.

Everything about Mom screams neat and tidy, from the sharp bun on her head to her wrinkle-free airline company uniform.

She shouldn't have work tonight.

"The vet has him on a diet," she says.

That's right. He went from a cat to a slab of lard, and now poor Pickles must endure timed feedings, special diet formulas, and walks on Mom's treadmill—with bacon dangled in front of his nose as bribery, of course.

"Until he stops biting me for food, I'm feeding him." I place the can on the ground.

Mom bends down and snatches the cat food. "Until you have a job and can pay for his check-ups, we're listening to the vet."

I roll my eyes and snicker when Pickles sharpens his claws on her pant legs. Mom pretends the needle pricks don't hurt, but her slight wince reveals everything. Pickles whines pitifully for the smelly meat chunks.

Mom puts the can in the fridge before she approaches me. She wraps me in a tight hug. I'm a bit put off by her sudden show of affection. Something's up.

"I have bad news." She releases her hold. "Work asked if I could come in. You're staying with your dad tonight."

"Seriously!" I smack my head.

Staying with Dad means I'll be working in the restaurant he owns. He always has me taking customer orders, chopping onions, or running the dishwashing station.

Mom and Dad split soon after I was born. It was a mutual decision. They were better off as friends. For my sake, they agreed to always live within driving distance of one another. Mom rents out a tiny apartment in the only affordable complex in Neiwood, and Dad lives above the restaurant he built.

I know things could be worse, like having parents who hate each other or always seeing one parent but not the other, but I feel like a hot potato tossed to whoever is least inconvenienced. If Mom has to cover someone's shift, I'm sent to Dad. If Dad has a big catering event, I'm given back to Mom. Nothing is ever consistent.

"We're leaving in exactly thirty minutes," Mom says.

I groan but know better than to argue with her before her work shift. I grab my overnight bag from the closet by the front door and head to my bedroom.

I swear there's a bed and dresser in here somewhere. You just have to push aside the clothes, makeup palettes, takeout boxes, and the deflated flamingo pool floaty that Maggie got me on the first day of summer. Posters of Elijah Nole plaster the wall, and I keep a plastic fork he used at school—which I swiped when he wasn't looking—in a shadow box next to where I sleep.

I'm not crazy. Loads of people keep things from their favorite celebrity. Who wouldn't want the napkin used by Robert Downey Jr. or one of Emma Watson's tossed socks?

Climbing Mt. Everest to my closet, I sift through the few clean clothes that remain on hooks. My clothes are nothing but designer name brands, scavenged from thrift shops down in Berkley and Hollywood. They are, of course, decade-old castoffs, donated by people who can afford the latest designer trends.

Mom and I make the six-hour drive to southern California every August before the new school year. The journey is to compensate for her refusal to spend three hundred dollars on a pair of black leggings or five hundred dollars for ripped jeans. She fails to understand the power of a brand name.

Oh, I *wish* I could buy the latest David Silk Collection, my all-time favorite brand. Even a simple headband will suffice. All I want is something new off the shelf, freshly wrapped in tissue paper, and placed inside a black paper bag with the gold engraved initials DSC.

Is that too much to ask?

I stuff a few outfits into the duffle bag and grab the blush satchel-purse that doubles as my school bag. I sling everything over my shoulder just as Mom barges in.

"Ever heard of knocking?" I snipe.

She scoffs at the state of my room. "Candice! I told you to clean over the weekend!"

"I did!" I lift my chin. "I organized underneath my bed." It's true. I pulled out everything and dispersed them evenly around my room in different piles.

"Is—is that broken glass in the corner?" she gasps. "Do you know how dangerous broken glass is? You need to clean that up right now!"

"Talk to the elves."

"I can't even . . ." She rubs the bridge of her nose. "Cleaning your room was our agreement for hanging out with Maggie today. That and your homework. You at least finished that, right?"

"Of course!" Nope.

"And you studied for your make-up math test tomorrow? The one you missed when you had the flu?"

"Yes." Also no.

Mom checks her phone. "We're running late!" she says, clapping her hands at me like I'm some sort of fly. She shoos me out of the apartment.

I hardly notice the moldy smell of the passenger seat seeping into my pants, or a drip of water from the leak in the roof of Mom's van. All I can think about, as we putter across downtown Neiwood, is Mrs. Gulligan. I'm not prepared for Mom's impromptu work shift.

What if she tries contacting Mom when I can't get to her phone?

Eventually, we reach the crossroad of Pinegrove and Auburn, just outside of downtown. Dad's restaurant is impossible to miss. While all the other buildings in Neiwood are old and faded, the Calico Oyster resembles a double-decker yacht with a sleek exterior and a rainbow of hanging lights on the boat's bow. Drinks are served in colorful fishbowls with polka dot straws and mini umbrellas, and the Japanese-Mexican fusion cuisine is purposely served on mismatched, tropical-themed dishes.

We squeeze through the crowded parking lot and pull around to the back of the building. A chair props open the door to the kitchen, the sound of clanking pots, oil frying, and chatting customers clear in the background. On cue, Dad pokes his head through the back door, waving as he walks out to greet us.

If I could preserve Dad in a jar, it would consist of chili peppers, sweat, a love for Elvis, and fifteen years behind the grill. He wears a chef jacket splattered with cooking wine. Tattoos of vegetables, knives, and all things culinary form sleeves down to his wrists. Dad has black hair, caterpillar eyebrows, and fogged up glasses from the kitchen's humidity. He doesn't need his eyes to cook, though. It's all muscle memory.

"Perfect timing!" he says as Mom rolls down the window.

"You got my message?" she asks.

"Don't worry. I have the perfect job for her." He winks before opening my door. "C'mon, up and at 'em."

I unbuckle and reluctantly get out. "You know, I'm pretty sure there's a law against child labor," I say.

"Not when their parents are their employers," Dad quips.

"Don't forget this," Mom chimes. She passes the plastic jail box with my phone through the window.

For a split second, I think she's talking to me. Is she lifting my grounding? My heart nearly bursts, thinking I have the coolest Mom, and I reach out to take it.

Dad swoops in and snatches my phone.

He waggles a finger at me. "Not 'til you finish that test."

I deflate, pinching my lips to the side. Great. They've already conspired.

Mom and Dad want to talk privately, so they motion me to the back of the van. As I grab my school bag and duffle, I lean around the corner to listen.

"The passcode for the jail box is 3156," Mom mutters, and I bite my lip to keep from grinning. My parents think they're sneaky, but I'm always one step ahead of them.

"How long will you be gone?" Dad asks.

"I won't be in touch until tomorrow morning, and I won't be home until tomorrow night. I'm working a flight to Atlanta."

I freeze. She's going out of town? Of all the times she's called to cover a flight, it has to be this week? Five days before the Fall Equinox Dance? This is bad. Really, really bad. An asteroid-striking-the-Earth bad.

I won't be there to intercept Mrs. Gulligan's emails or calls. There must be something I can do . . . like block Mrs. Gulligan.

Yes! That's it! Why have I never thought of it before! If I block Mrs. Gulligan's email, then there will be no chance that she can reach Mom. Seriously, this is the greatest idea since, well, sliced bread!

I slam the van trunk shut, reminding my parents that I'm still present before sauntering up to the driver's window.

"Mom?" I say in the sweetest voice I can muster. "I need to borrow your phone really quick. For school, of course."

"Use your dad's. I'm running late," she says.

"But—"

Mom shakes her head and says goodbye. She rolls up the window, leaving me face-to-face with my nervous reflection.

As Mom squeezes through the parking lot, I wish a pothole would open and swallow her van. Too bad, Dad had the lot redone a few months ago. It's still new and shiny and has yet to experience northern California's wet, eroding winter.

Soon, Mom is gone.

What am I going to do now? I wasn't expecting her to go out of town!

A hand rests heavily on my shoulder, and Dad spins me around. "Let's get started, shall we?" He pushes me toward the back door.

The kitchen of the Calico Oyster is spacious, consisting entirely of stainless-steel counters and appliances. The air tastes of garlic, spices, and roasting meat. Steam from the dishwasher station mutes the lighting, as a line of cooks move at inhuman speed, frying food and plating dishes. The noise is deafening.

Dad leads me to the office, a small room with framed photos of the Calico Oyster during construction. In one picture, a three-year-old version of me wears a hardhat and reflector vest, wielding a shovel over her head and growling at the camera. Another photo shows us standing in front of the newly finished restaurant. Dad and I hold up a massive banner announcing the grand opening.

Dad drags his swivel chair to a foldable table shoved in the corner. He sets down a calculator, some scratch paper, and a stack of algebra study guides.

"You can go upstairs after you finish each question," he says.

"That's totally not fair."

"Your mother and I have to get you to study, somehow."

"At least let me have my phone, so I can look up videos on problems I don't understand." And so I can sneak into Mom's email. I've activated my phone, so it won't send Mom a login notification. Blocking Mrs. Gulligan might actually work!

"Not a chance," he says. "I'm taking your phone and your things upstairs to the apartment. Use my computer if you have to, but not for anything except math. I know how to look up the history even if you try to delete it."

I groan and sit down. Dad gives me a thumbs up and leaves the office, taking my belongings with him. The corner of the purple jail box case peaks out of his pants pocket.

I sit unmoving, glaring at where Dad had once stood. Movement draws my eye to a circular window above the desk. Dad appears outside and climbs the stairs leading to our apartment.

He takes tiny living to the next level. The space is half the size of Mom's. My room is barely a closet, crammed with a bunk bed, storage cubbies underneath, and a pull-down, wall-mounted desk. Who needs a big place when you spend 99.9% of your time at work? At least, that's Dad's logic.

I pick up one of the math worksheets and scan the problems, but I'm not actually reading them. How am I supposed to stop Mrs. Gulligan from contacting Mom now? I can't use

Dad's computer—not without alerting Mom. And what about the phone calls?

I glance at the analog clock on the wall. 6:45 pm. My stomach grumbles, reminding me that I haven't had dinner yet. Surely, it's too late on a Sunday for Mrs. Gulligan to phone anyone's parents. Even if she does, Dad won't check his missed calls until after work. It's better to call the restaurant when trying to get a hold of him. As for Mom, she turns her phone's settings to Do Not Disturb for work, only accepting calls from me, Dad, or my aunt. As long as Mrs. Gulligan doesn't contact Mom between now and when she clocks in, I should be fine.

It's an email from the stubborn English teacher I worry about.

I need to get my phone.

I smack the worksheets against the table and stand up. My chair rolls across the room and claps against the wall. I dart to the office door and look through the peephole. The cooks are focused intensely on their jobs. You would think it's easy to sneak behind them, but they have some sort of sixth sense about who's in the kitchen. If I try, they will notice my escape attempt and rat me out to Dad.

Speaking of my jailor, Dad slips back into the kitchen and resumes his position in front of his stove, monitoring the wine-induced flames spewing from the pan. I squint at his pocket and note the absence of my phone's jail box. At least he's true to his word. Dad hid my phone upstairs. If I can sneak out of the office, I can use the code I overheard and steal my phone back.

The question is how?

A light breeze grazes the back of my neck, and I turn around. Above the desk, the window is cracked open.

Bingo. My ticket out.

I push aside Dad's keyboard and piles of paperwork and hoist myself onto the desk. I stand slowly, the legs of the desk wobbling, until I'm eye-level with the window. I observe the opening before pushing the glass as far out as it will go with its metal hinge.

I poke my head out first. I'm several feet above the back lot, but there's a pipe to my right that I can grab to pull myself out. I test the width of the window and squeeze more of my upper body out. My exposed arm catches on the inside of the frame. I could wriggle though if I wanted to shave off a few layers of skin.

I retreat into the office and lower myself to the ground, scowling at the window. How do you reduce friction for an object that's stuck?

Dad used soap when I crammed my finger into a bolt washer a few years ago. I doubt he keeps soap in the office, but maybe there's something else I can use.

I open the desk drawers and dig through the chaos of mail, phone cords, and knick-knacks. I come across a container of hand cream and cheer. Unscrewing the lid, I dip my finger into the yellow goo.

This will work!

Scooping out a large glob, I lather the lotion over my shoulders. I apply some to my exposed neck and back before adding a generous layer to the window frame.

Feeling nice and greasy, I lift myself up and through the window. My shoulders slip through with ease. Success! The hand cream works! I'm a genius. Maybe not in school, but definitely where it matters in the real world.

I slap the slanted exterior of the faux boat, reaching for the pipe. I grasp the copper—just barely, fingers slippery with hand cream residue—and haul more of my body out.

My hips catch on the frame this time. The metal edge digs painfully into my flesh. I squirm, pulling on the bar with all my might. For a moment, I'm afraid that I'm stuck. I can already imagine the morning news. *"Firefighters sawed a thirteen-year-old girl from a local restaurant window."* But then my hips begin to move, and I pop out of the window like a cork from a bottle.

I fall to the ground, arms outstretched and cushioning the rest of my body.

"Ouch!" I cry when pieces of gravel jab my skin.

Slowly standing, I shake off the pieces of rock and cringe form where dust clings to the hand cream I lathered all over my body. I scraped my elbow during the fall, and blood pools into dozens of tiny droplets. I wipe off the wound on my pants.

This will all be worth it now that I'm free and can get to my phone.

"3156." I whisper the jail box passcode under my breath as I thunder up the outside stairs.

Dad's living space is a little bigger than a studio apartment with a granite-top kitchenette, a den swamped with food magazines, and a loft above a heated-tile bathroom. Trays of microgreens grow on the kitchen table, which we only ever use on holidays. Massive windows take up nearly every wall, providing a 360-degree view of Neiwood.

I climb the ladder to Dad's loft, yank the bed comforter and sheets aside, and lift the mattress. He thinks he's clever hiding stuff here, but I discovered this spot when I was, like, seven years old.

I spot the plastic jail box in the corner and snatch it up. Biting my lip, I enter the code and grin as it chirps an affirmation. I open the top latch and shake out my phone. Joy floods my chest like I've been reunited with a lost limb. I press my thumb against the fingerprint sensor, but the screen remains black.

Dead.

I groan, lowering myself from the loft and searching the apartment for a charger. After tearing through all the clutter, I flop on the couch and rap my fingers against the armrest. The manufacturer's logo flashes on the screen.

"C'mon, c'mon," I mumble impatiently.

The home screen flashes a picture of me and Maggie shoving s'mores into each other's mouths, followed by my app shortcuts. My phone warms, notifications chiming as the dozens of texts I missed over the last few days come in. Most of them are from Maggie, but there are few from some unknown numbers that arrived less than an hour ago. All of them ask about my "famous cousin."

"I didn't think word of that lie would spread so fast," I mutter.

I push that worry aside, though. I'll come up with some sort of solution, like I always do, after I deal with Mrs. Gulligan.

I log into Mom's email and search the trash folder for my teacher's last email. When it pulls up, I right-click Mrs. Gulligan's email address. An action menu appears, and at the bottom is "Block Sender." My pulse surges. I hold my breath as my finger hovers over the screen. I close my eyes as I tap the icon, feeling as though this is too good to be true.

Cracking an eyelid, I see another notification appear. It warns that if I block Mrs. Gulligan's email, all previous and future emails from her will be deleted.

Do you want to continue?

Yes! A million times, yes!

I watch as all the emails of Mrs. Gulligan vanish.

I did it. I actually did it!

I squeal, jumping to my feet before I twirl and dance a jig. The movement causes my phone to unplug. Realizing my mistake, I quickly insert the cord once more. Of course, charging the phone won't matter since I have to put it back in the jail box under Dad's mattress.

I exhale deeply, willing my vibrating body to calm down. I don't have a lot of time, since Dad could check the office any minute. I read the messages from Maggie, shoot a couple of responses, and return my phone where I found it. Outside of the apartment, I take another deep breath. I catch whiffs of the hot fudge Dad drizzles on his fried ice cream, and I decide that's what victory smells like.

"Why did I not think of blocking Mrs. Gulligan's email sooner!" I smack my forehead, descending the stairs with an ear-splitting grin. "No stubborn English teacher can outwit me!"

"Candice."

The Southern drawl startles me, and I trip down the final two steps. I catch myself on the railing, steadying my feet on the gravel, and whip my head to the last person on Earth I ever want to see.

Mrs. Gulligan.

She's standing in the parking lot of the Calico Oyster in a black, pineapple-themed maxi dress and massive straw sunhat. What are the odds that she shows up here at the exact time I block her?

Maybe she is a witch, after all.

I shiver, feeling like someone dumped ice water on me. My stomach churns so violently that I wonder if it's going to roll right out of my body.

Am I in a dream?

Did I eat bad cheese curds at the beach BBQ?

Is Mrs. Gulligan actually standing in front of me?

"Let's chat, shall we?" Mrs. Gulligan's voice is sickly-sweet. "I'd love to hear all about this *stubborn English teacher* you have outwitted."

FOUR
Mrs. Gulligan the Witch

The wait staff gives me odd looks when they pass the table where Mrs. Gulligan and I sit. I grimace at Barbara, a college-age server with dyed blue hair, when she approaches and asks if everything is alright. It's not normal for me to eat a meal in the dining area. Usually, Dad makes me eat in the office, unless it's a special occasion.

I pray they don't mention anything to Dad.

As Mrs. Gulligan browses the menu, acting like she didn't just catch me trying to stop her from contacting my parents, I can't help but notice how much she looks like a gerbil.

Oversized glasses mount her paunchy cheeks, magnifying her abnormally circular eyes. She is as dimwitted as a gerbil, too. She's constantly calling the school's IT guy for help turning on the projector, and she never remembers her students' names, referring to each of us as "my dear" or "sweetheart." A headache starts to throb above my right eye from the overpowering stench of black licorice surrounding her. Sometimes, I wonder if she bathes in the putrid candy or adds it to a perfume meant to make her students gag.

"Are you ordering food, deary?" Mrs. Gulligan asks.

I straighten, back twinging. How can she expect me to eat after being caught? All my plans are ruined! When Mom and Dad find out, I can kiss my chances of attending the dance with Elijah goodbye.

"I suppose we've stalled enough." Mrs. Gulligan closes the menu and sets it on the table. Propping her elbows on the wood, she rests her chin on her clasped hands and leans forward. "Before we address your failed endeavor to prevent communication between me and your parents, let's talk about the reason why I'm contacting them in the first place.

"I'm worried about your missing homework and failed assignments. I know it's still the beginning of the semester, but you risk not passing my class if this habit continues."

I bite the inside of my cheek to refrain from rolling my eyes. This situation isn't new. Teachers come to me all the time with their fake concerns over my poor grades. In reality, they couldn't care less. They count down the days until they can boot troubled students onto the next teacher in the grade up.

"Candice?" she says, and I realize I missed something she said.

"It's Candy," I correct, instantly regretting it. Now is not the time for cheekiness. She doesn't seem phased, though.

"Now that I know you've been interfering with my emails and phone calls, I'm afraid I must hand this situation over to the principal," she says.

"No!" I spring to my feet, belly knocking the table.

Water sloshes out of my glass and a few customers at nearby tables turn their attention toward us. Out of the corner of my eye, I see Barbara whisper something to another server before they both disappear into the back kitchen. This is not good.

Mrs. Gulligan raises a brow. "If you want to avoid an uncomfortable talk with the principal, I need you to tell me the truth about why you've only submitted half of this year's schoolwork."

She clasps her hands together and waits. I freeze, weighing my options. No matter which route I take, truth or silence, my parents will know.

Mrs. Gulligan wants the truth? Fine. I bite my tongue. Hard. Tears spring to my eyes and I take several shaky breaths before dropping my head.

"You're right. I haven't been completely honest with you," I sob, shoulders shaking for extra effect. "Truth is, I've been so distracted."

Mrs. Gulligan's seat creaks. A gentle hand rests on my shoulder.

"By what, deary?" she asks tenderly.

I almost feel guilty.

Almost.

"I haven't told anyone, so I don't know where to start," I gasp.

"Take a deep breath," she says. "You can tell me anything."

I look up, lip quivering. "It's my mother. She's got this new boyfriend—Brady is his name. You see, they're always out late. Like coming-home-the-next-day late. My mom's a whole new person, partying all the time. I think that's why she lost her job. We had to move in with her boyfriend. Since then, she acts like I don't exist."

The story comes out in one jumbled breath. Mrs. Gulligan's mouth parts in shock, causing her cheeks to sag even further, which seems impossible. Her thumb rubs circles where she still touches my shoulder.

Before she can say anything, I whimper, "And with my mom's boyfriend in the picture, I can't help but think about . . . my dad."

"Your dad?"

I nod and brush my hair behind my ears. "My parents split when I was a toddler. I've only seen him on three or four occasions since then. The last time we met up was four years ago. My mom told me that he made a lot of bad choices. Now, he's living on the streets who knows where." I take another shaky breath.

"So the restaurant you mentioned he owns . . ." She waits for an explanation.

"Doesn't exist." I stare at my hands. I do everything in my power not to break character and burst out laughing. If only Mrs. Gulligan knew we were sitting in my dad's restaurant at this very moment.

"Can you see why I've been so distracted?" I ask, looking up at her with teary eyes.

Mrs. Gulligan sniffs. She reaches over, yanks a napkin from a dispenser, and dabs the moisture forming around her eyes. She scoots out of the booth and walks to my side, pulling me up into a tight, flabby-armed hug

"Oh, sweetheart! Of course I can see why you've been so distracted," she cries. "I'm so, so sorry you are going through this."

We stay in that position for a solid, awkward minute. I pull away, wipe the trail of half-dried tears from my cheeks, and return to my seat.

"I haven't been able to focus in any of my classes, honestly," I say. "That's also why I told you all those stories."

She takes another tissue. "Have you spoken to anyone about this? The school counselor? She can talk to your mother for you. Of course, you'd have to let me contact your parents. No more blocking emails."

"No!" I blurt.

Mrs. Gulligan tilts her head.

"It's just—" *Think, Candy, think!* "—I want to to try talking to my mom first and solve this myself before involving anyone else. It's why I haven't told anyone, not even my best friend."

Mrs. Gulligan's back straightens. She puffs out her chest as though entrusted with secret documents from the Pentagon. She snatches another napkin and rummages her purse for a pen. She quickly jots something down.

"I understand you want to keep this to yourself, but it's okay to ask for help. Here." She passes the napkin to me. "Normally, I'm absolutely against giving out my personal phone number to students, but I'll make an exception just this once. If you ever need anything—and I mean anything—don't hesitate to give me a call."

True to her word, Mrs. Gulligan's phone number sprawls the yellow paper in vibrant red ink. I gape at the numbers. This is definitely a dream.

"Candice!" Dad booms, emerging from the kitchen.

Bile rises up my throat. Sweat forms over my brow, and my sense of hearing seems to heighten. Every chatter and bout of laughter from the other customers sends my heart into a thudding frenzy. My wrists and neck pulse painfully.

No. Oh, please no.

Dad stops at our table. He wipes his hands clean on a rag before extending one. When Mrs. Gulligan shakes it, the restaurant seems to slowly cave in until I'm trapped in a dark box with little air. I almost dry heave.

"Who is your lovely friend?" he asks me.

Mrs. Gulligan chuckles, bringing a hand to her cheek. "I'm her English teacher."

"No kidding? I'm Candy's dad, John."

I gulp as Mrs. Gulligan's smile slowly falls. She snaps her head toward me.

Gone is Mrs. Gulligan's gerbil face. Instead, I stare into the dangerous eyes of a vulture. The black licorice stench that clings to her skin intensifies, mixing with something foul and rotting. The world stands abnormally still, the air electric. Dad, the wait staff, and the customers are all motionless, like someone clicked the pause button during a movie.

Like magic.

Not a sound interrupts Mrs. Gulligan as she speaks, her voice cruel and venomous.

"You walk a dangerous path, Candice. Your words and actions affect everyone around you. They can either create or destroy your life. It is time you learn lies have consequences," she says before gliding out of the restaurant.

Just as the door slams, the black licorice smell disappearing, the world jumps back to life.

FIVE

I Die In A Bathroom

"What just happened?" Dad stares between his hand and Mrs. Gulligan's empty spot. "There was a woman here, right? Your English teacher? Am I hallucinating?"

"I need to use the bathroom!" I exclaim.

I spring to my feet, and this time my hip hits the table hard enough to knock my glass over. Orange soda spills, dripping on Dad's shoes. He curses and jumps away. I run past him and the tables of diners watching the scene.

"C-Candice!" Dad calls, but I ignore him.

Both individual bathrooms are occupied when I arrive. I hop from foot to foot until one finally opens, and I barge around the man. Locking the door, I run my hands through my hair and step backwards until my back hits the sink.

"Mrs. Gulligan is a witch, you know." Maggie's words play in my mind.

No, no, no! I will not fall for some fantastical rumor. Witches are a myth. Nothing more. What happened between me and Mrs. Gulligan is simple: I succumbed to shock. I was shocked that Mrs. Gulligan showed up at the exact moment I blocked her. Shocked that she invited me to eat dinner and explain my poor grades. And shocked that Dad ruined everything.

That lie was perfect! My best one yet!

For once in my life, I don't know what to do next.

I avoid the mirror as I wash my hands, splashing water on my face. I let a few drops slide down my cheeks and watch them fall into the basin before I turn the faucet off.

Water continues to pour out.

"What the heck?" I twist the handle again.

The flow intensifies. The sink fills up faster than it can drain. Within seconds, the water spills over the counter and onto the floor.

"Dad!" I yell, stepping back from the rapidly expanding puddle.

I grab the doorknob and turn.

Click.

It's stuck.

Click. Click. Click.

Not a budge.

How is this possible? How can I be locked *inside* a bathroom?

The faucet rockets off the sink, smacking the ceiling before landing in the toilet. I scream. A fountain of water sprays into the air, and I gasp as it sloshes onto my sneakers.

"Help me!" I pound the door as hard as I can. "The bathroom is flooding!"

Either everyone in the restaurant is ignoring me or something mystical is preventing them from hearing the commotion. I shout, jiggling the knob until the growing pool reaches my waist. Soon, I'm lifted until my feet no longer touch the ground. Gasping and paddling my way to the counter, rising water already covers the faucet hole, muffling the spray as I climb onto the counter and hold onto the light fixture for dear life.

I'm in a dream. That's the only logical explanation for what's happening. Lucid dreaming, I think it's called? Maggie explained the phenomenon when we were reading about sleep cycles in science class. It occurs when a person realizes they are in a dream and, in a way, have some control over what is going on.

I raise my fingers to my temple, channeling Charles Xavier, and close my eyes. "Please form a magic drain and get rid of this water," I beg. "Please don't let me die in a bathroom. Not like this."

It doesn't work.

Standing on the counter proves useless. Only a small gap of air remains, forcing me to tread once again. The top of my head scrapes against the ceiling. I open my mouth to wail for Dad, but water steals my voice.

This is it. I'm going to die.

The light above the mirror explodes in a firework of red-hot sparks. The bathroom goes dark.

***

"AHHHHHHHHHHHH!" I shoot up from bed, my blanket twisting around my body and covering my face. I thrash like a fish caught in a net. Powerful coughs shake my frame, trying to expel the heaviness of inhaled water from my lungs. A deep, sharp ache blossoms in my chest, one that comes from holding your breath for too long. I relish the feeling, though.

Pain is a sign you're awake. That you're alive.

I spend the next couple of minutes inhaling and exhaling before I notice something's off. Black licorice lingers in the air. My mind flashes briefly to Mrs. Gulligan, and I open my eyes.

And gasp.

I'm lying on a queen-sized bed in a room that is obviously not my own. The walls are painted a gradient of pastel pink, purple, and teal. The massive bedroom is decorated with white fur rugs, sequined pillows, and fairy lights trickling from the ceiling. A cluster of paper pompoms form a cloud above a marble-top dresser, and a bookshelf in the corner hosts several trophies, medals, and stuffed animals.

The bedroom reminds me of a birthday cake. Whoever sleeps here is the luckiest person on

Earth because this is literally my dream room. Everything is pristine and tidy, not a crumb or strewn garment on the floor. The shelves and drawers are even labeled with chalk paint stickers.

How did I get here? Am I still in a dream?

I don't have much time to ponder. Footsteps plod outside the closed door. I slap a hand over my mouth as someone knocks, jiggling the handle. Thankfully, the door is locked.

A deep, unfamiliar voice causes the hairs on my arms to rise.

"What's with all the racket?"

"W-Who's there?" I demand with a strangled gasp.

"Who do you think?" The man sounds annoyed.

"I don't know!" I squeak.

A horrifying thought crosses my mind. *I have been kidnapped.*

That's the only logical explanation as to why I woke up in a stranger's bedroom. But when did it happen? And how? The last thing I remember is the bathroom flooding.

"Keep it down. Your mother is sleeping," he warns, voice growing faint. The floorboards creak as he walks away.

My mother? Was she kidnapped too?

Several minutes pass before I work up the courage to move. I slip out of bed, legs trembling, and try not to freak out that I'm wearing unfamiliar silk pajamas. Someone must have dressed me while I was sleeping. I shiver.

Stay calm, I tell myself, *stay cool—cool like cucumbers.* The biggest mistake I can make right now is panicking. I just need to keep a level head and figure out what is going on and—

Who am I kidding?

I dart to the French windows and yank aside the sheer white curtains. A misty breeze cools my flustered cheeks, and I get my first glimpse of rolling waves rushing over amber sand before slinking back out to Morgan Bay. Froggy horns of faraway boats echo from beyond a wall of morning fog. I'm still in Neiwood, that much I know. In fact, I'm not far from the beach where Maggie and I collect garbage. I can see the abandoned lighthouse from here.

The window is on the third floor of an apartment complex. The exterior wall is made of stacked stones with deep grooves that I can easily climb down. Bushes line the base of the building and will, hopefully, add some sort of cushion if I fall.

Lifting myself up, I hoist my legs out the window and twist my body so I face the siding. I lower myself until my bare toes catch on a cool ledge and slowly start to descend. I make it down a few feet, but I stop.

Mom.

I can't just leave her alone in the apartment with some stranger. What if she's hurt? What if the stranger takes her to a different location while I'm getting help? What if she ends up like her Saturday night murder documentaries?

I change course and climb back to the bedroom. When my feet *thump* against solid ground, I scan for a weapon I can use for self-defense. The plethora of fluffy pillows and stuffed animals are disheartening, but a trophy on the display shelf catches my eye. I wield it like a baseball bat and creep to the door, pressing my ear against it.

Muffled voices overlap music before both are interrupted by a round of sitcom laughter. The TV is on. I can't tell if someone is watching it or just has a show on as background noise. I can't hear any movement.

I count to three, hold my breath, unlock the door, and slowly turn the knob.

The bedroom leads to an apartment den. It's dark. The curtains are drawn and only the light from the television provides visibility. The den has an edgy, modern vibe with sleek black furniture and a massive abstract painting that stretches into the adjacent kitchen.

I scan the den for my kidnapper.

I almost miss a human-shaped lump underneath a blanket on the couch. A head pokes out on one end, spilling coils of red-dyed hair. Mascara smudges the skin underneath her eyes, and lipstick smears her cheeks, giving her a striking resemblance to the Joker. Something about her seems so familiar, though. The woman shifts, and I realize why.

She's my mom.

I creep over to her side, shocked by her sudden change in appearance. I gently pull back the blanket. She's wearing the shortest black dress known to man, along with a pair of blood orange stilettos. Glitter covers her body from head to toe, and a neon paper bracelet wraps around her wrist.

What in the world happened to her?

"Mom!" I shake her shoulder. "Mom, wake up! We've been kidnapped!"

She snorts, pushing herself up and yawning noisily. I get a whiff of her revolting breath and nearly gag. It smells like peanut butter mixed with something foul. I yank her wrist urgently, but she slaps my hand away. She falls back onto the couch with an "oof" and brings a pillow to her face.

"Go away," Mom muffles.

I try to remove the pillow, but her grip is too strong.

"You're being ridiculous!" I say. "Don't you realize the situation we're in? We've been kidnapped! Your hair is tomato red! And—"

Someone coughs behind me. I jump from my crouched position with a sharp scream. Trophy still in hand, I lift it over my head and get ready to throw.

The man raises his hands in mock surrender. He wears a white tank top and boxers. His skin shimmers with glitter just like Mom's, and an orange band dangles from his wrist, too. He has sandy hair and droopy brown eyes. A stingray tattoo swims down his bicep and forearm.

"Stay back!" I warn.

"Samantha, your daughter is acting stranger than usual," he says.

He knows Mom's name. *How* does he know Mom's name? And why is he acting like he knows my normal behaviors?

Our stand-off lasts until the man rolls his eyes and heads to the kitchen. He rummages through the fridge and pulls out a carton of milk. He takes a long, noisy swig before slamming it on the counter and setting up a bowl for some cereal from the pantry.

The trophy slips from my hand, clattering against the floor, and I drop down next to Mom. My lips graze her ear.

"Who is that guy?" I whisper.

She rouses enough to stare incredulously.

"Are you talking about Brady?" Her throat is hoarse.

Why does that name sound so familiar? I've heard it somewhere recently.

"Yes, him—Brady—the guy who abducted us. We need to get out of here," I urge.

"Candice." She rubs the bridge of her nose. "It's too early for your wild imagination. You know Brady."

"No, I don't! You've never mentioned Brady before, or introduced us, or brought me to his place." Goosebumps form on my arms and legs as panic rushes through me. "Mom, something is seriously wrong here."

"The only thing wrong here is you waking me up before nine with some bogus story," she snipes.

Okay, who replaced Mom with an alien? Unless her work shift goes past midnight, she is always up by 5:30 a.m. on the dot. Mom is half robot. I'm the one she usually has to drag out of bed before the school bell rings.

I shake my head. That isn't the point. She is treating our situation with no urgency. I need to know where we are, how we got here, and who the man in the kitchen is!

"I'm not imagining things! First, I was drowning in our bathroom, then I woke up in a stranger's bedroom, and now I find you here dressed like that and acting like everything is normal." I gesture around the apartment.

"Do you hear yourself?" Mom blinks.

"Just tell me what's going on!" I beg.

Mom groans and rolls her back to me, pulling the covers over her head. I jostle her shoulder, but soft snores tell me she has fallen back to sleep. Conversation over.

Brady returns from the kitchen, and my fingers twitch for the trophy on the ground. He stands behind, face twisted in an unimpressed scowl. Up close, he smells of leather and woody deodorant.

"You missed the bus," he says.

School is the last of my concerns, right now. Plus, how would he know anything about my bus route?

"Get dressed so I can take you to school."

"No!" I cry.

There is absolutely no way I'm leaving Mom alone with this nutcase.

"Samantha," Brady groans. "Deal with your daughter." He goes back to the kitchen and pulls out a blender. He mixes strawberries, peanut butter, and—dare I say—asparagus with ice to make a smoothie. Disgusting!

My shoulders sag, relieved that Mom and I are somewhat alone again. But before I can say anything, Mom gives a moan of annoyance.

"Please, Candice. Just do what Brady says without an argument—just this once."

"But—"

"Don't argue. Go. To. School."

I jerk back. Her words spit like hot grease. Mom never talks to me in that tone. Not even when she caught me with the fake vomit.

My lip quivers from both hurt and fear. I reluctantly retreat back to the birthday cake bedroom. I glance, one last time, at my already half-asleep mother and wonder if she's actually the woman who birthed me. With a fractured breath, I lock the door, wedging the desk chair underneath the door handle for extra protection.

To Whom It May Concern,

This is the Last Will & Testament of Candice Lynn Sky. If the Neiwood News hasn't reported this already, my mother and I have been kidnapped. The culprit, a man named Brady, hypnotized my mother into believing everything is perfectly normal. It's not.

I am writing this letter in case I don't make it out of this deceivingly nice apartment. The following are a list of my wishes and demands

1. Joe's Hawaiian Ice is to name a signature shaved ice bowl after me.

2. Elijah Nole is to sing at my funeral, preferably his hit single, "We Stop For No One."

3. Magnolia Middle School is to make an honorary speech about me at the Fall Equinox Dance and paint a mural of my face on the gymnasium wall.

Thank you for fulfilling these wishes.

Sincerely,

Candy Sky

SIX
The Golden Closet

I chomp on my pen, wondering if I should rewrite the letter with more demands. The ones listed aren't too inconvenient. If I add more, whoever finds this letter might pick and choose which demands to honor. Three seems like a good number. Modest, too. It's quite mature of me to show such restraint.

Carefully folding the letter, I clutch it to my chest and scan the room for the perfect hiding spot. I don't want Brady discovering it, but I also don't want police missing the letter if they investigate the apartment.

Underneath the bed is too obvious. The dresser is a better option. I can stuff it under some socks, making just the corner of the paper visible.

Inside the drawers, I'm surprised to find nothing but art supplies, old textbooks, and other knick-knacks. There are no clothes in sight. I shake a jar of colorful marbles, noting how similar they are to the ones I've collected over the years. I leaf through several pamphlets for Spelling Bee competitions and swim meets. I come across something that steals my breath, and I drop the letter.

It's a picture of me and Mom standing in front of a coffee stand. I was five at the time and remember the day well, the first time Mom let me try "coffee," which was actually hot cocoa she convinced me was a mocha. However, instead of holding coffee cups in this picture, we're holding brown-green smoothies.

Strange.

The picture is glued to the front of a photo album that I have never seen before. I open the cover and discover dozens of snapshots slipped into plastic pocket protectors. Like the photo on the cover, all of the pictures are different than the memories I have of them. During our camping trip to the Redwood National and State Parks when I was six, Mom and I slept in a discounted tent, but the photo shows us lounging in a luxurious camper. And instead of posing in front of thrift shops with bags of hand-me-downs during our once-a-year shopping sprees in Hollywood and Berkley, Mom and I pose in front of various designer boutiques.

I rub my eyes, pinching my cheek when I see myself standing in front of a David Silk Collection store, holding a black bag with gold tissue paper. Just the sight causes my heart to flutter.

I stop halfway through the album, shocked by a face I never expected to see. Laurell. She waves at the camera, her other arm draped across my shoulders. We must be ten or eleven, and both of us are dripping wet in swimsuits by the local pool.

That can't be possible. I've never met Laurell, aside from rumors and passing her in the hallways, before today at the beach. Or was that yesterday? I still don't know what day it is.

My confusion grows when I look at the next photograph. Once again, the picture is of me and Laurell. This time, we're dressed in Princess outfits—her as Cinderella and me as Rapunzel—hugging each other in front of Disney World's whimsical gates. Our faces are smeared with powdered sugar and strawberry syrup from the funnel cake in our hands. How old are we? Eight?

I *remember* this. Mom and Dad saved up for a family pass, surprising me at the end of the third grade. Best of all, they allowed me to take one friend.

I chose Maggie.

I have this exact picture pinned to my bedroom wall, except I'm posing with Maggie. Not Laurell.

What is going on? Did Brady photoshop these? Why is Laurell in these photos? Where is Maggie? The rest of the album provided no more clues, only a surprising lack of Maggie.

And Dad.

I go back to the beginning and observe each photo again. There's none of him or the restaurant. Why? Is Brady playing mind games?

There must be something here that sheds light on the situation. I set the album aside and pull another item from the drawer at random. It's a graded algebra test.

With a "100%" next to my name written on the top.

I bring it close to my face, nose brushing the paper. The handwriting is mine, but I've never earned a hundred percent in math. I peer back at the drawer. Another test gleams with a perfect score and a smiley face next to it. And under that one, another. This time from history class. Flipping through the sheets, I find at least two dozen tests and essays with top marks next to my name.

An album of people and events I don't remember? Tests with perfect grades? My dream room? Now I know I've woken up in an alternate universe.

Wait a minute.

Time stopped in the restaurant. I drowned in the bathroom and woke up in my dream room. I found Mom after she obviously spent the whole night partying. Add to all that the perfect grades and endless trophies, and Maggie had to be right.

Mrs. Gulligan is a witch.

I finally realize why Brady is so familiar. He's from the lie I told Mrs. Gulligan about my parents. He's the boyfriend I made up for Mom.

Does this mean my English teacher used some sort of spell to make my lies come true?

A rap at the door startles me. I scramble to put everything back in the drawer, standing up quickly. I grab a crystal cup from the trophy shelf, noting that its heavy weight and jagged sides could do some serious damage. A plaque on the bottom reads *1st Place Individual Medley.* I have no idea what that means.

"Candice." Brady's tone is sharp. "Are you done getting dressed?"

I choke, no words coming out. I'm too scared to speak.

"You better not have gone back to bed." He jiggles the door handle.

The thought of him barging into the room sparks what little courage I have.

"Almost done," I squeak, bringing a hand up to muffle a cough. The words feel rough, like rusted gears stuttering to turn.

"Ten more minutes. I'm already running late for work."

I will investigate more of the drawers later. With a police escort, preferably. Although, I doubt they will believe me when I say I've woken up in a world where my lies have come true.

I check the closet for something to wear, wanting to get out of these pajamas as soon as possible. I don't know how I got into them, nor do I want to know.

Flicking on the light, I step inside and whistle at the size of the space. A twin bed, a desk, and a large dresser could fit inside. Neatly pressed clothes hang on double-tiered racks, and a shelf on the back wall displays dozens of shoes and accessories.

I gasp as I realize everything in the closet is a designer brand.

I look over my shoulder, half expecting the owner to appear and yell at me to get out. When that doesn't happen, I sift through the clothes eagerly. I find Calvin Klein sportswear sets, Lululemon dresses and leggings, Michael Kors handbags, and NYDJ jeans—the list goes on and on! I freeze when I spot something poking out from behind a coral Georgia Cloud sundress.

Star emojis materialize as I pull the outfit off the hanger and hold it up. I almost do not believe what I am holding. In my hands, I feel the softness of the powder blue romper with tiny periwinkle polka dots. The initials DSC are engraved in gold above the right hip bone. The outfit is from this year's David Silk Collection, my favorite designer brand in the entire world.

I have to try it on.

I check the tag on the back, note that it's in my size, and begin to laugh maniacally.

As I step into the romper, goosebumps form where the lace straps glide over my skin. I tie the sash around my waist and close my eyes. I wonder if this is how the models feel whenever they wear the latest and hottest designer trends, like a new luxury car that everyone stops to admire.

With each stroke of my thumb against the fabric, my problems melt away like popsicles in the summer sun. I feel free and exquisite. Royal, even.

Racing out of the closet, I jump in front of the full-body mirror on the wall and twirl. The legs of the romper flare out, and I squeal at the sight.

I can't believe this is happening. I can't believe I am wearing something from the David Silk Collection! If I did die in the bathroom and this is the result, then I think I'm okay with that.

The only thing better than this would be, well, if Elijah Nole was my boyfriend.

I spend the next few minutes trying on different shoes and scarves to pair with the romper. Everything fits perfectly, as though they were handpicked just for me. I settle for a soft peach scarf that I tie loosely around my neck and a pair of lattice sandals. A headband of white daisies rests on my head like a tiara.

I hardly recognize the girl staring back in the mirror. She seems so much older and more mature—a celebrity heading for a photo shoot rather than a girl heading off to middle school.

Another knock on the door interrupts me, and I force myself to look away from the mirror.

"Yes?" I answer.

"Time to go," Brady announces.

Right. I forgot about him.

"How will I get to school?" I ask, stomach flip-flopping.

"How do you think? I'm driving."

Oh, heck no.

"I want Mom to take me," I demand. Maybe this is my opportunity to get both of us out of this apartment, even if it does have the greatest closet in the world.

"Trust me, she's not getting up anytime soon," he snorts.

"But—"

"I don't have time to argue. I need to be at work in less than twenty minutes. You are getting in the car now or else I'm taking your phone away."

"My phone?" I whisper, a little confused that he would use such an ordinary tactic against me. "Do you know where my phone is?"

"You left it last night on the charging pad in the kitchen," he says. "It's been blowing up like crazy all morning. I'm holding onto it until you get in the car."

Knowing Brady is a fragment of a lie helps ease my fears, but he's still a stranger. I don't trust him, but I'm desperate to find out what other lies have come true. I'll risk the ride to school. Plus, if I have my phone and Brady tries anything, I can call 911.

"I'll be out in five minutes," I say.

SEVEN
The World Flip-Flops

Brady leads me through the apartment complex's impossibly luxurious hallways, with crown molding on golden walls, raindrop crystal chandeliers, and velvet curtains. We enter a massive lobby with pedestal marble pillars. A man in a black suit greets us through the glass window of a kiosk. Behind him are dozens of metal mailboxes.

Once outside, we head to one of the covered carports. Brady presses his remote and a silver sports car chirps. I blink, impressed.

Instead of normal doors, the entire side of the car automatically folds above the roof and reveals the interior. Brady climbs inside, and the car hums to life without him having to turn the key in the ignition. He motions for me to hurry, and I scurry around to the other side of the car to the backseat—the one furthest away from Brady.

"You're not sitting up front?" he asks, combing fingers through his hair while checking himself out in the rearview mirror.

I ignore his question and focus on the car's synthetic cedar smell. The seats practically mold my body, leaving me comfortable and drowsy. A tablet-like control pad monitors each cushion's individual temperature, and a TV hangs from the roof for the back row. If this were any other situation, I would be screaming with excitement.

This is a million times better than Mom's beat-up, moldy van!

Eventually, Brady rolls his eyes and pulls out of the carport. We drive in tense, awkward silence. I grip the handle of my door, preparing my escape if he hints at taking me somewhere other than Magnolia Middle School. I don't imagine he would harm me. He didn't hurt me in my lie. But I can't be too cautious. Brady turns on the radio to some talk show, and I'm grateful for the noise.

We arrive at the parent drop-off lane ten minutes later, true to Brady's word. He parks with the car running, and I rip off my seatbelt and jump outside, relieved that we're no longer in close proximity. My legs itch to run inside the brick building. I want to learn what other lies have come true, but I hesitate.

My last period of the day is English with Mrs. Gulligan. She and I aren't exactly clicking right now. I don't know how she'll react when I stroll into her classroom like I didn't lie to her for the past month—like I don't know she's a witch.

"Here." Brady hands me a piece of paper through his open window. "Give this to the office. I don't want them calling me about your attendance."

I stare down at a note claiming I had a doctor's appointment this morning. Occasionally, my parents fib when excusing my tardiness, so I'm not surprised by the pass. The signatures on the bottom, however, catch me off guard. Brady Wilcox and Samantha Sky. Who does Brady think he is?

At least now I know that today is Monday, meaning there are only four more days until the Fall Equinox Dance. That's still happening in this world, right?

The car honks, and I squeak.

"Quit daydreaming!" Brady leans over the passenger seat and thrusts a phone into my hands. "I don't have all day!"

I smile. A phone! *My* phone! I could almost kiss the screen.

Brady peels out of the lane, zipping down the road before I can say goodbye. Not that I wanted to. I unlock my phone as I walk toward the school's front entrance.

I stop mid-step. Instead of the picture of Maggie and me stuffing our mouths with s'mores, I look down at a photo of Laurell and I in front of two horses, one solid white and one dusted with cinnamon speckles. We wear matching t-shirts with a local equestrian camp's logo on the front.

If that's not enough to surprise me, the notification bar at the top of the screen reveals thirty-four text messages and three missed phone calls. I nearly choke when I see all of them are from Laurell. Half of the texts are her asking me where I am, with strings of emojis that probably translate into messages, but I'm too shocked to decipher their meanings. I know for a fact I never lied about Laurell being my friend, not that I'm complaining. She's the most popular girl in school! Her friendship has always felt like a pipedream.

What else has Mrs. Gulligan changed about my life? Is there more to her spell than simply making my lies come true?

My phone vibrates, and a new text arrives.

Remember our plans for this afternoon.

The text is from someone named Yolanda. I reread the sender's name again and again, bringing my phone closer each time. One unbelievable realization purges my mind of all other thoughts.

Yolanda Nox is real.

My lie about having a famous cousin is also now true, and I have plans with her this afternoon. I don't know how to process this information. Everything is so overwhelming!

I scroll through our text messages, reading our conversations about her talk show. In one, she asks me to keep her show a secret, but other texts from Laurell and several unknown numbers indicate that I broke that promise. Hopefully, she isn't too mad at me for that.

I can't find anything else about our plans, but a quick search of my recent phone calls reveal that we talked last night for almost an hour. Well, that doesn't help. We probably discussed it then. I should ask her for clarification.

I send a quick text: *Remind me?*

I wait a few seconds for a response, but nothing arrives.

Nervously, I take a deep breath of warm September air. I grip Brady's note harder than I should, crumpling the paper into a wad, and continue into the school.

I stride past the school's seal mascot and metal detectors, walking over to the secretary's desk between the main office and the rest of the school. Mrs. Ocampo snacks on carrot sticks while reading something on her computer. She reminds me of a bear—large with curly brown locks stacking on top of her head. She wears a rose-themed blouse and black slacks.

Mrs. Ocampo greets me with a bright smile. "Hello, Candice! What can I do for you?"

I force a smile and hand over the note from Brady.

"A doctor's appointment, huh?" She takes the excuse and begins typing on her computer. "How did it go?"

"It went—"

A violent cough seizes my body before I can finish my sentence. I bring my hand to my throat. It's as though I accidentally inhaled food or swallowed water down the wrong hole. The coughs continue. Tears form in the corners of my eyes, and snot begins to dribble from my nose. In the midst of it all, I smell something putrid.

Black licorice.

"You sound awful! Are you sick? Is that why you had a doctor's appointment today?" Mrs. Ocampo hands me a tissue.

"I'm fine," I say between hacks, wiping my face.

"Would you like to see the nurse?"

I shake my head no, the coughs subsiding. The smell of black licorice fades, and I know that coughing fit was not a coincidence. It felt artificial—unnatural. Like something purposely clogged my throat so no words could come out.

Why does the smell of black licorice keep popping up?

The school bell rings.

"Well, it looks like third period has started. Better head to class," Mrs. Ocampo says.

"Right, thanks." I hunch my shoulders and scurry away.

As soon as I turn the corner, out of sight of the office, I slow to a stop and lean against the wall for support. An itch lingers at the back of my throat. I have no doubt that Mrs. Gulligan's spell has a physical effect on me.

I need to figure out this spell, and fast. I need to think like Maggie. What would she do in this situation?

She'd probably document all the strange occurrences caused by the curse, creating a spreadsheet comparing her findings to the lies I've told. Everything would be typed and color coded, probably turned into some sort of experiment. Maggie is such an overachiever.

I don't have Maggie's level of focus or dedication, but a list might prove handy. I will create one in class. And afterward, I'll find Maggie by her locker, and we can solve Mrs. Gulligan's spell together.

EIGHT
The Cursed World

Cursed World

- I live in a super nice apartment with my mother and a man named Brady.
- I have a dream room and a dream closet.
- I'm friends with Laurell.
- I have a famous cousin named Yolanda Nox.

I've decided to name whatever reality I'm currently in the "Cursed World." I need names for before and after Mrs. Gulligan's spell, otherwise I'm going to lose my mind with all the confusion. Cursed World is simple enough. Plus, "Spell World" doesn't sound right.

Just as third period ends, I finish the list and tuck it into my notebook. I exit the classroom with everyone else, receiving a few waves from girls who normally don't notice me. Liking this new spotlight, I smile and wave back.

I'm halfway to Maggie's locker when a high-pitch whine drifts over the passing period chaos.

"CAND-EE!"

That voice. Why is it so familiar?

I turn around in time to see Laurell shove her way through the river of our classmates. She reaches my side and matches my pace, walking shoulder to shoulder like we're friends. I falter mid-step, but the flow of students pushes me along.

"I cannot believe you went to your next class without me!" Laurell nudges me with her elbow.

"S-Sorry," I say, hands shaking with excitement. I can't believe the most popular girl in school, Elijah Nole's cousin, is my best friend. If I ignore Brady and the weird coughing fit, the Cursed World is more like my Dream World.

"I have something that will make you happy," Laurell cut through my thoughts. "I've been trying to give it to you all morning, but I couldn't find you."

"I was late for school," I say.

"That explains it." Laurell holds out an envelope with my name written on the back. "This is from Elijah. He's at his recording studio for a couple of days and won't be back at school until Friday. Otherwise, he would have given you this himself."

"From Elijah?" I barely breathe, staring hungrily at the letter.

Laurell waggles her eyebrows. "Someone's boyfriend needs a partner for the dance."

No. Freaking. Way.

I swipe the envelope from her fingers. My body radiates with excitement as I thumb Elijah's surprisingly elegant cursive handwriting. *Elijah and I are going out.* I vaguely remember telling my dad that we were dating. Could it be that my ultimate dream came true? Slowly, I open the flap and pull out a piece of paper that had obviously been torn from the bottom of a notebook. Gulping, I read the message.

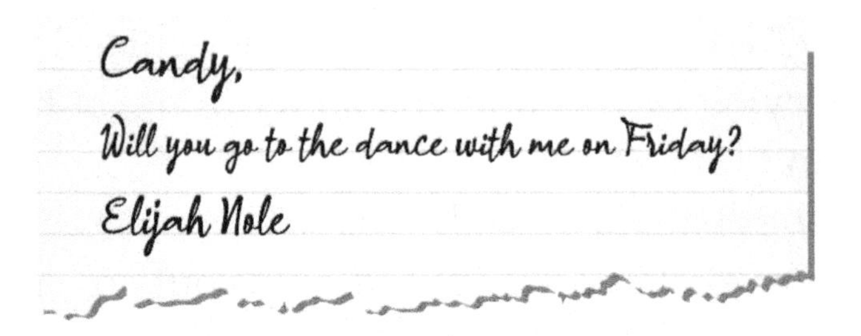
Candy,
Will you go to the dance with me on Friday?
Elijah Nole

"Yes!" I shout, fist-pumping the air. "Yes, yes, yes!"

Laurell nudges her elbow against my arm, eyes darting back and forth. "Candy, you're causing a scene."

I realize we're standing in the middle of the hallway, forcing everyone to go around us. They give me funny looks, but I don't care. I jump up and down in a circle, laughing until tears spring in my eyes. Laurell backs away.

"I'm leaving for class before you embarrass me anymore," she says. "See you at lunch . . . . Hopefully, by then you're composed."

I barely utter a goodbye. I fixate on the cursive handwriting sprawling the lined paper. Elijah Nole is my boyfriend. *Elijah Nole is my boyfriend!* My mind chants the news over and over again until I'm singing it down the hallway, kicking my heels as I skip.

For the rest of the day, I wonder how we met? Who asked who out? Were we friends beforehand, or was our relationship sudden? Have we gone on any dates? Have we kissed? I barely register Laurell dragging me to her table for lunch or locking arms with her during each passing period. I'm on cloud nine!

Before I know it, my last period arrives. Only when I reach the door of my English class does the problem hit me. My mood fizzes down to panic.

I forgot about Mrs. Gulligan.

There's no way I can simply walk into her classroom after discovering she is a witch. What if she realizes she botched the spell? Despite Brady and the coughing fit, things are great. She might reverse everything! Or worse! She might slap me with an *actual* curse! Then Elijah Nole wouldn't be my boyfriend!

The bell rings, and I jump. Thuds from teachers shutting their doors echo around me.

One boy sails down the hallway, footsteps pounding the tile floor and papers flying out of his backpack, hoping a few seconds won't warrant a tardy attendance.

"Candy."

A young, beautiful teacher emerges from Mrs. Gulligan's classroom. She has shimmering black hair, light brown skin, and a pink pantsuit that reminds me of Elle Woods from *Legally Blonde*. Gold corset heels add three inches to her height. The woman could be a business executive or, perhaps, a celebrity. I'm a bit awestruck by her appearance.

"This is the first time you have ever been late to class," she says. "Is everything alright?"

"Uh," I stare dumbly.

The woman places a hand on my forehead. She hums, deep in thought. I'm too baffled by her apparent closeness to me—or the Cursed World's Candy, I guess—to say or do anything. After a few seconds, she drops her hand and shakes her head.

"You don't feel warm. Perhaps you're having an off day?"

"Y-Yeah."

Who is this woman?

"No worries. Go sit down. I'll let this slide, but just this once."

At least she's reasonable.

My usual spot is taken. We don't have assigned seating, but there's an unspoken agreement between students that the desk you choose at the beginning of the year is yours until the end. Unfortunately, the only empty spot is at the back of the classroom, next to Sayer Lafayette.

I slowly approach Sayer, who's slumped over in his seat. What if the rumors are true about him being cursed? I don't see any oozing boils on his face, nor is he wearing the gloves that everyone says protects him from turning money into leaves.

I open and close my mouth, pondering how to ask. What if he is like everyone else? What if he also doesn't realize there's a difference between the Cursed World and My World?

The young woman shuts the door, walks to the front of the classroom, and welcomes another day to the "end-of-summer madness." There's an excited murmur, and I catch a few whispers about the dance this Friday.

Why is no one mentioning the fact that we have a sub?

As the young woman starts the class, I lean over to Sayer.

"Where's Mrs. Gulligan?" I ask.

He blinks at me, his mouth dropping open. "You know Mrs. Gulligan?"

"Duh," I say, "she's our English teacher."

Sayer seems taken aback; eyebrows scrunched together.

"You gonna answer my question?" I ask, wondering why he's acting so strange.

"I honestly have no idea," he says. "Yesterday, she existed. But today, it's like she fell off the face of the Earth." Sayer points to the woman. "Everyone insists that Mrs. Garcia is our English teacher."

"No freaking way." I slap my forehead.

"You're the first person who's mentioned Mrs. Gulligan," he confirms. "I even went through past yearbooks in the library and couldn't find her. Like I said, it's as though she never existed."

"Th-That's fantastic!"

"Fantastic?" He sounds confused. "Don't you want to figure out what happened to her?" Sayer rubs his hands together, staring at them intently.

"Absolutely not!" So far, the Cursed World is the best thing that has ever happened to me. I have no desire to see Mrs. Gulligan, possibly break the curse, and ruin my chance with Elijah at the dance. Not to mention going back means facing my parents after lying about my grades and sabotaging Mrs. Gulligan from contacting them. I'll take Brady and the coughing fits any day over returning to the mess waiting for me at home.

"Okay, okay. Tell me one more time. There's no Mrs. Gulligan?" I can't believe my luck. I need to hear it again. "She's gone?"

"I guess so," he says with a frown.

I jump from my seat, knocking my bag to the ground and gaining everyone's attention.

"YES!"

NINE
A Little Black Credit Card

When the final bell rings and everyone spills out of Magnolia Middle School, I'm utterly exhausted. Navigating the Cursed World is more work than I thought, and I want nothing more than to climb into bed in the birthday cake room. *My* birthday cake room.

Laurell finds me in the hallway, and we walk to the pick-up circle together. She prattles on about the Fall Equinox Dance. Apparently, Elijah Nole's parents—my *boyfriend's* parents—

already booked a limo for us. I grin and nod along, pulse quickening with anticipation.

I wait until Laurell's ride pulls up, and she climbs inside a massive pickup truck. She rolls down the window and leans her body outside. As the truck begins to move, she blows me a kiss.

"Mom and I will pick you up for school tomorrow!" she calls.

Awesome. Now, I don't have to worry about grouchy Brady driving me to school again, even if he has the nicest car on earth.

I watch as Laurell sits back and rolls her window closed. I wonder which lie changed her from a stranger to my best friend. Only Maggie has held that position, but I can definitely make room for someone like Laurell Mayflower Reynolds.

That reminds me, I haven't seen Maggie all day. Then again, every time I tried finding her, something new about the Cursed World distracted me.

I wait until the truck turns a corner before taking out my phone. I frown when the home screen appears.

For some reason, Maggie no longer has a speed dial icon. Laurell does. Another small detail to add to my list. I search my contact list for Maggie's number. I can't find it. Unfortunately, I don't know her number by heart.

Blowing out a frustrated breath, I vow to find her first thing tomorrow morning. She will probably be in her usual spot in the study hall.

I look up when someone honks a salmon-color VW Beetle convertible's horn. I don't know what year the car is, but I can tell it's vintage. The hood pops open and reveals a storage compartment.

Impressed, I whistle.

A woman in her twenties adjusts her sunglasses in the mirror. She has a sharp black bob and strikingly pronounced cheek bones. A white crop top shows off her chest and stomach. Something about her screams movie star. Judging by a group of girls pointing at the woman, I'm not far off.

She notices me staring, grins widely, and waves me over.

At that moment, I realize this beautiful woman is Yolanda Nox.

My legs move before my brain can siphon the shock, and I open the door to her convertible and sit inside. Yolanda's floral perfume is obnoxiously strong, but everything else about her is the definition of perfection.

"You'll have more leg room if you put your backpack in the trunk," Yolanda says, voice fruity and confident. I let her take my purse and store it in the front of the beetle. She shuts the hood and gets back in the driver's seat.

Yolanda turns to me. "What are you staring at?"

"N-Nothing," I say. I force myself to look away.

"Judging by your text, you forgot we made plans today." She carefully inches out of the pick-up circle.

"Sorry about that," I say. "I had a lot going on."

We turn down a road that takes us out of Neiwood. Most people use this route to get to the freeway. Curious, I shift in my seat, looking outside.

"You've been talking about the dance for months. I'm surprised this slipped your mind," she says.

I laugh awkwardly. I wish she would stop teasing and give me a hint as to where we're going.

"How was school? Anything interesting happen?" Yolanda asks.

"Not rea—"

I cough, loud and hacking, unable to stop until tears are flowing from my eyes. The smell of black licorice is prominent. Yolanda reaches over and pats my back. She grabs an iced coffee from the drink holder and hands it over. I sip the chocolate-flavored drink, feeling lipstick residue on the straw. Grossed out by sharing with a stranger—even if Candy of the Cursed World is close to Yolanda—I decline when she insists that I finish off the iced coffee.

"Swallow a bug?" Yolanda asks jokingly.

I shrug, not trusting myself to talk. Mrs. Gulligan's spell must be sensitive if trivial lies cause that strong of a reaction. Does this mean I can't lie at all? That almost seems impossible, even for someone as honest as Maggie. Can I even exaggerate? I'll need to think about my words before I say them. The last thing I want is to cause another coughing fit by saying something as benign as "I'm starving" or "I walked a thousand miles to school."

The last of the black licorice evaporates, and I relax.

The drive takes almost an hour, and we kill time by singing to Elijah's album. An hour into the drive, we pull over at a fancy food truck and enjoy overpriced but delicious ice cream. Only when we exit the freeway and see the shimmery gold exterior of my favorite mall do I realize what Yolanda and I planned for today.

"Shopping!" I cheer.

"For the dance!" Yolanda says. She snags the first available parking spot.

The mall is a spider web of walkways branching out from a pavilion. There are three levels, two of which are for shopping and eating. The top level is a movie theater. Even though I've come to this mall countless times, I still get lost in the maze of stores. I have to check the directory constantly.

Yolanda, on the other hand, knows exactly where she's going. She zigzags through the crowds, turns several corners, and cuts through a tunnel behind a junction of escalators. We pop out in a walkway with only a few people, practically empty compared to the rest of the mall. A rectangular marble fountain runs down the center.

Yolanda stops in front of a small boutique. Black windows block us from seeing inside. A gold plaque above the door displays DSC in wispy cursive.

My breathing becomes ragged, and I clutch my purse as an anchor.

I, Candice Lynn Sky, am standing in front of a David Silk Collection's storefront.

I don't remember there being one at this mall—and believe me, I would have sniffed it out in a heartbeat. This must be another change caused by Mrs. Gulligan's curse.

I hold my breath as we pass through the doors. A security guard greets us from a small kiosk. The store is about the size of a small bedroom with a cozy couch and two armchairs centered around a glass coffee table. There are no racks of clothes. Instead, the far back wall contains floating shelves that display this year's handbags and accessories. If I didn't know better, I'd have thought I stepped into an upscale living room instead of a retail store.

"Welcome back, ladies!" a voice calls as a young Korean-American woman emerges from the stock room.

She wears a black business suit, her brown hair twisted in a spiral bun. Two leather-bound binders are tucked under her arm, and she hands each of us one, beckoning us over to the couch.

"May I get you two something to drink while you look through our catalog?" she asks. "We have both lemon-blueberry and plain water."

"Fruit water sounds amazing, thank you," I say, still in shock that I'm in a David Silk Collection boutique. Judging by the woman's greeting, this isn't the first time I—or rather Candy of the Cursed World—have been here.

Yolanda asks for fruit water too, and the clerk returns to the stockroom.

I trace my fingers along the binder's spine, goosebumps rising at the softness of the leather. I bite my lower lip and close my eyes as I debate whether I should look inside. I'm almost too nervous about what I might find.

Turning to the first page, I see models posing in many different scenes, wearing dresses that probably cost several thousand dollars. Pair them with the shoes, accessories, and jewelry, and the overall cost rises to the equivalent of a new car. I peruse their outfits, one piece at a time and take in everything from the barrettes in their hair to the tiny toe rings visible through their open-toed sandals.

I savor this moment as though it is the last piece of chocolate on Earth.

The clerk returns with crystal cups full of yellow-tinted water. She places them on the coasters on the coffee table before sitting in one of the chairs.

"What are you looking for today?" she asks.

Up close, I'm able to read her name tag. Aera. Her name sounds as fancy as the designer brand. I wonder if that's a requirement to work here—good looks, friendly attitude, and a unique name.

“My cousin here is looking for a dress.” Yolanda wraps an arm around my shoulder and tightens it into a sideways hug. “This Saturday is the Fall Equinox Dance at her school, and she has a very special date.”

"Oh! A date to a school dance!" The clerk beams. "How cute! Are you going out to dinner beforehand?"

"We haven’t decided yet,” I say, thinking I should ask Elijah later. “Maybe Dale’s Bowling Alley.” That’s where everyone in town goes on dates. Well, there or the Calico Oyster.

Hold up. With everything going on, I forgot about Dad. I swallow guiltily. Does the Calico Oyster exist in the Cursed World? My lie to

Mrs. Gulligan means that Dad is on the streets, homeless. If that's truly the case, I doubt he went to culinary school or had the idea for his beloved restaurant. I'll have to Google the Calico Oyster as soon as I'm done shopping.

"I remember my first school dance—prom of junior year." Yolanda joins the conversation, eyes growing distant and dreamy. Her plum lips part into a small smile. "We went out for dinner and a play beforehand. My date brought me flowers, and after the dance, we went to the beach where we walked under the moonlight."

"That sounds so romantic!" I say.

Yolanda coughs and fans her face, as though the breeze would disperse the memory from her mind. "It was lovely. Though, I have to admit bowling for a first date sounds like a lot more fun. First dances are special. Good or bad, the memory will stick with you for the rest of your life. Aim for fun rather than mainstream expectations. An honest daisy always trumps a bouquet of roses hiding a foul stench."

"Sounds like something my grandpa would say," Aera says, and I laugh.

Yolanda snaps her fingers. "Close! It's my grandmother's saying. She has a hundred and one years of wisdom she likes to dump on me whenever I visit."

I briefly wonder how we're related in this world. If Yolanda is my cousin, does that make her Mom's niece? I guess Aunt Becky is old enough to have a twenty-something-year-old daughter. In my world, she doesn't have any kids. Maybe she's from Dad's side. I don't know very much about his family.

When we finish browsing the binders, Aera whisks us out of the consultation room and to the back of the store. The stockroom is much larger than the front. Racks and racks of clothing mount the walls. Three mannequins—a man, a woman, and a teen—pose on a velvet stage in the center of the room.

Aera brings us to a line of fitting stalls that are split by a strange hexagonal contraption with metallic walls. It looks like a space pod you might see on the Sci-Fi channel.

I gasp. The walls of the room are all mirrored. I have only ever seen this setup in magazines and on *Young, Bold, and Beautiful.* I think I've died and gone to heaven.

Aera opens a changing stall curtain, and I step inside. She then fetches a flowing pink dress and passes it to me over the stall. The Vneck reveals more chest and stomach than it covers. It is beautiful, but it's not going to work. I try it on only because it belongs to David Silk's brand.

Whatever Mrs. Gulligan did, I hope the spell never wears out.

I move on to the next outfit, a purple power suit. I love the sophisticated look of the blazer and slacks in theory, but . . . not on me. I'm too short and scrawny. I look like a baby playing dress up in Mommy's clothing. Maybe in a few years?

The next dress is much more age appropriate. Unfortunately, it's hideous. The neon green color reminds me of a sour apple Jolly Rancher. For the first time in my entire life, I discover something in the David Silk Collection that I actually dislike.

More outfits arrive. Poor Aera hauls the clothes back and forth diligently. She offers a few suggestions to speed things up, but Yolanda and I are having too much fun. My cousin pretends to be a fashion judge, while I catwalk to the mirror and strike a pose. We giggle, and I sit next to Yolanda on a padded bench for a breather.

"I think I'm starting to understand what kind of style you're looking for," Yolanda says. "You want something classy but not over the top. Something to accentuate your features, not drown you out so all anybody notices is a nice dress. Am I right?"

"Yes!" Finally! Someone who gets me.

"I know the perfect dress," Aera chimes, before shooing me back into the stall. She returns a few minutes later. "Don't look once you put this on. Surprise yourself in the mirror," she instructs.

I'm handed a yellow dress with an airy, violet skirt that goes all the way down to my ankles. The fabric is soft and breathable. The color is like a lemon popsicle on a hot day.

I adore this dress.

As I step out of the stall, the dress embracing my body like a second layer of skin, Yolanda and Aera hand me a fuzzy purse and a pair of sandals.

"Stunning!" Yolanda exclaims, and I choke up.

She pushes me to the mirror. I twirl, causing the dozens of other Candys in the mirror to spin.

I've never felt more beautiful. I want to remember wearing this dress for the rest of my life.

"I'm guessing this is the one you want to buy?" Yolanda asks.

"It is," I breathe.

The excitement is short-lived. How am I supposed to pay for the dress? I was kinda under the impression that Yolanda would be treating me.

I check the price tag.

$1,599.99.

"Holy cannoli!" I lift my armpits, searching for sweat stains and smudges, making sure I didn't damage the fabric while trying it on. I hop out of the mirrored room to take off the dress.

I've been so focused on trying on clothes from my favorite designer brand that I forgot to consider the cost. This is a designer store. Of course the prices are out of this world.

"Shall I ring you up?" Aera asks as she exits the changing stall.

Before I can respond, Aera takes the dress from my hands and heads out of the stockroom. Yolanda is hot on her trail. I hesitate, not wanting to upset Aera after she worked so hard to find me the perfect dress.

I can pretend I left my wallet at home. Although, that means I will have to tell a lie, and so far in the Cursed World, I'm magically forbidden from doing so.

Yolanda calls my name.

The security guard watches me intently as I trudge toward the register. Aera gently folds the dress in a glittery tissue paper. I watch numbly as she gently places it in a black shopping bag, engraved with gold lettering. It's a bag I've wanted to hold for longer than I can remember.

Yolanda's arm slinks through mine, and she draws me to her side. She rambles about all the different ways I could style my hair and which eyeshadows go with the dress. She is completely oblivious to the sweat cooling my skin. I pinch the collar of my romper and fan myself.

Aera taps on the register and says, "Your total comes to $1,719.99."

My eyes bulge. "I thought it was $1,599.99"

"Sales tax," she says.

"O-Oh."

"Cash or card?"

"Huh?" Air forces itself past my constricted throat.

"How are you going to pay?" Aera asks politely.

I glance at Yolanda who gestures to my purse. Maybe I have enough money in this world for the dress? I haven't exactly investigated everything in my possession.

Digging for my baby blue wallet, I unzip it slowly. Normally, I only carry my student ID and leftover gaming tickets from when Maggie and I hit the bowling alley. This wallet, however, contains dozens of coffee stamp cards, gift cards to various stores, and a black credit card issued to Brady Wilcox. Directly below his name in the same textured print is my name.

I stare at it in disbelief. Aera coughs, drawing my attention, and she asks "cash or card" again.

"C-Card," I stutter.

I slowly slip the card out, noticing the faint sound of its corners gliding against the fabric of the pocket holder. I hold it out to Aera, but she points to the card reader on the counter. I insert the card into the reader, and the screen asks if I approve the amount. I scribble my signature and then tap the confirmation.

My body tenses, and I brace myself.

The screen flashes green.

Approved.

Cursed World

- I live in a super nice apartment with my mother and a man named Brady.
- I have a dream room and a dream closet.
- I'm ~~friends~~ best friends with Laurell.
- I have a famous cousin named Yolanda Nox.
- ELIJAH NOLE IS MY BOYFRIEND!
- ELIJAH NOLE IS MY BOYFRIEND!
- ELIJAH NOLE IS MY BOYFRIEND!
  This totally deserved three bullet points.
- I'M GOING TO THE DANCE WITH ELIJAH NOLE!
- Mrs. Gulligan does not exist.
- I'm a frequent shopper at David Silk Collection.
- I have a credit card!

TEN

Unwanted Visitors

Yolanda drops me off at Brady's place, and luckily I remember his apartment number. I prance through the hallways, swinging my David Silk Collection bag for everyone to see. In the elevator, I pull my new dress out, hold it to my body, and spin on my toes. I laugh excitedly, feeling the happiest I've been since, well, finding out that I'm dating Elijah Nole.

Now, I have no doubt that Mrs. Gulligan botched her spell. My lies may have come true, but so far, they're mostly working in my favor.

It figures that the first witch I meet is as ditsy as her English teacher persona.

Entering the apartment, I kick off my shoes and flick on the lights. The TV and coffee pot are off, and I don't hear anything from the master bedroom. Mom and Brady must be off somewhere doing who knows what.

I relax now that I know I don't have to deal with Brady.

A yawn reminds me of how late it is. I'm utterly exhausted. My encounter with Mrs. Gulligan feels like a lifetime ago, and I want nothing more than to curl under my covers and fall asleep.

In my bedroom, I gently place the DSC bag on the desk. I admire the shiny gold lettering before I change into fuzzy pink pajamas and crawl into bed. Since Mom is gone, I leave the bedroom light on.

I plug my phone into its charger, placing it on the nightstand, before I bring the covers up to my chin. I close my eyes, ready for sleep.

I want tomorrow to come as soon as possible.

Patter. Patter. Patter.

My eyes snap open as tiny footsteps scamper underneath my bed. They sound like rat feet. I shiver, pulling the blanket over my head. If I feel a hairy, germ-infested rodent run over me, I'm going to scream.

"Candy Sky tells a lie! Now she'll eat humble pie!"

I almost miss the tiny voice singing my name. Someone is in the room with me. My arms and legs tingle as adrenaline seeps through my body. I hold my breath and listen.

The singing continues.

"Candy Sky tells a lie! Now she'll eat humble pie!"

Something slides off my desk and clatters to the ground. A second voice joins the mantra. Then a third. Then a fourth. For a moment, I wonder if I fell asleep and this is all a dream. Tiny people don't exist, and they certainly wouldn't be invading my bedroom.

Unless . . .

I smack my hand against my head, recalling all the times I told Mom that elves destroyed my room. The fib was more of a joke than a lie, but I guess that doesn't matter in the Cursed World.

How powerful is Mrs. Gulligan's magic?

The blanket lifts just enough for two yellow eyes and a bulbous, warty nose to peek inside.

Tendrils of braided white beard hair spill through the opening. The creature's face is the size of my thumb, his features as small as a grain of rice.

An elf.

I scream in terror. I kick my legs, the blankets and tiny man falling to the ground, and propel myself across the bed. I yelp when my back hits the wall. The following silence magnifies my heaving breaths. Papers flutter down from the ceiling, and a few trophies are knocked off the shelf. I'm alone, except for the small lump struggling underneath my covers.

I pinch my arm, checking that I'm not dreaming.

"Get this off of me!" A muffled voice grunts.

Movement from the corner of my eye catches my attention. Several small figures emerge from hiding spots throughout the room and run to their friend's aid. At least seven elves, all wearing either burlap overalls or dresses, grasp the edge of the blanket and lift it up.

The elf who had greeted me clambers out. He's older and fatter than the rest, beard longer and more extravagant. He wears a bottle cap for a hat with two hairy ears curled downward.

What looks like a butter knife is clipped to his back.

The elf brushes the wrinkles from his outfit, muttering as he hobbles toward me.

Part of me worries he might attack. Who knows what these elves are capable of? My hand inches toward a pillow, grabbing a corner. I'll whack them if they show any sign of ill intent.

"My name is Brutus Hurst." The elf mocks me with a deep bow. "And you're Candy the Cursed."

"Uh . . ." My mouth parts open, speechless. I honestly have no idea what to say to the six-inch tall creature.

He tugs a thread from the rug and begins flossing his teeth. "Not as smart as you claim." I wince when he spits.

"Are you really elves?" I ask, watching as he tosses the thread aside.

"*Are you really elves*?" he mimics. "Of course we are elves. What else would we be?"

"Elves are supposed to be cute and sweet," I say. "You look like a bunch of old, cranky garden gnomes."

He scoffs. "How dare you lump us with those dirty, worm-eating tree huggers!"

"Did Mrs. Gulligan send you?"

His lips curl into a smile. The elf spins toward his companions and dances around them. He repeats his song.

"Candy Sky tells a lie! Now she'll eat humble pie!"

The other elves join in, looping their arms together and dancing a jig in a circle. Their voices grow higher and whinier, and I cover my ears when it becomes too annoying to bear. Soon, the song penetrates my fingers as I try to block the sound, and I reach for the pillow once more.

Aiming for Brutus Hurst, I throw the pillow and hit the elf and two of his companions out of the circle. They hit the bedroom door.

The singing stops. The elves gape at me before turning toward their fallen friends. They unsheathe makeshift bows and arrows, pointing their weapons at me.

I gulp. I think I made a big mistake.

Brutus Hurst sputters as he pushes the pillow away. His face is blotched red and purple from anger. He pinches his thumb and index finger together and brings them to his lips. A high-pitch whistle causes the whole room to freeze.

The white-bearded elf raises his hand in the air. "Elves, let's party!"

The elves bellow a battle cry and explode in every which direction. One scales the wall, jumps on the hanging lights, and swings through the air while whooping wildly. Another climbs the trophy shelf and stops to admire its reflection before shoving the cup off, cackling when the crystal shatters into jagged pieces.

The closet door flies open. Clothes rip off the hangers and shoot across the room. A pair of heels stab my arm, and I leap to my feet with a cry. Grabbing another pillow, I swing it randomly, deflecting the projectiles.

The mattress dips next to my feet. Brutus Hurst appears, wielding his butter knife. He twirls his body and swings his knife around and around before hitting the back of my calf.

The knife is dull, and the force doesn't even dent my skin, but I screech at his close proximity. I jump over his head and off the bed. My ankle twists when I hit the floor, the bone zinging with pain, and I collapse to the ground.

I push myself up, groaning, and I feel something cold and sticky on my left cheek.

Someone chomps on something, smacking their mouth loudly in my ear. I look over to find a younger looking elf, wearing homemade goggles over his eyes. In his hand is a pink roll of Hubba Bubba bubble tape. Where did he find that? The elf grins, sugary juices dripping down his chin, and then spits the gum at my forehead.

"Gross!" I wipe the slimy wad off of my face.

I have to get out of here, especially before Brutus Hurst finishes his descent down the bed and takes another whack at me.

The elf chewing gum bulges his cheeks as he prepares another round of fire. I roll toward the door and spring to my feet. Ignoring the sharp pain lancing up my leg, I gape at the chaos.

Gone is the organized, pristine birthday cake room. Now, I'm practically standing in the middle of my old room, a disaster of clothes, homework, and junk covering every inch of the floor. I watch with despair as the elves yank the drawers open, snatch the papers from inside, and throw them in the air. They flutter down like tree leaves.

Or 52-card pick up, I recall grimly.

"What's this?" I hear Brutus Hurst and turn as he crinkles wrapping paper.

My heart lurches in my throat. He's digging through my David Silk Collection shopping bag! I can't let him destroy my new dress!

"Give me that!" I lunge toward him.

Brutus Hurst dodges, slapping my hand away. I'm surprised by the tiny elf's strength. He waggles his finger at me.

"Ah, ah, ah! I didn't hear the magic word," he says.

"I'm not going to say 'please' for a dress that belongs to me!" I say.

I search the room for something to help rescue my beloved dress. A black rubber blade sticks out from underneath the bed. My paddle! I dodge another shoe aimed at my head and dive for the oar. I note the carrier for my inflatable board next to it. Extending the shaft to its fullest length, I lower the blade like a hockey stick.

Brutus Hurst holds a fistful of purple fabric in his grubby fingers. His eyes widen as I shout and run toward him with a giant paddle in hand. He throws the bag away just as I scoop him up with the blade and stick-handle him toward the closet door.

Lifting the oar behind me, I swipe it forward and slapshot Brutus Hurst. He howls, holding his bum, and lands in the closet. I slam the door shut and step back, chest heaving.

The elves in the room calm. They stare with wide eyes at where Brutus Hurst disappeared. The one swinging from the lights drops onto the bed with a huff. I note a tremble of fear in the elf chewing gum. Good. I hope they are afraid of me!

I shift stances, jutting my paddle out threateningly.

"If you don't want to end up like your friend, I suggest you get in the closet before I make you," I say.

The elves clamber forward. They race around my legs and toward the closet. I open the door just enough for them to squeeze through. I count seven. If I include Brutus Hurst, that means eight elves terrorized me. I think that's all of them.

With the elves trapped, I throw the paddle aside and hurry toward the dresser. I push the clunky, marble-top furniture until it barricades the door. That should keep them contained.

Collapsing to the ground, I take a moment to catch my breath. I stare around in disbelief. If it were not for the state of the room or the muffled chatter coming through the walls, I wouldn't have believed this actually happened.

Shakily, I crawl to my nightstand, careful to avoid the shards of glass from the broken trophies. Thankfully, my phone is still plugged into the outlet, undisturbed by the elves. I clutch it to my chest and lean against the bed. The screen lights up, but I hesitate.

I want to call someone, but the question is who. I've tried Mom's number throughout the day to check on her, but she never answered. A gut feeling tells me I'll go straight to voicemail if I call her now, too. Based on the lie I told Mrs. Gulligan, Dad is MIA. Laurell and Elijah are both out of the question. I can't imagine their reactions if I told them about the elves. They wouldn't believe me.

The only person I want to talk to is Maggie.

She would know what to do in this situation, but she is also missing in the Cursed World.

I gather my phone and then the David Silk Collection bag. Unfortunately, Brutus Hurst ripped the side. I'm a little bummed that I can't display the bag somewhere in my room, but at least the dress is safe and in perfect condition.

I step over the elves' rubble and exit the bedroom. I'll have to sleep on the couch tonight, not that I believe I'll get a wink.

ELEVEN
Sailfish

I dream of elves braiding my hair with gum when a hand pats my face, waking me. I groan and try swatting at whoever is interrupting my sleep. My back is stiff from the firm cushion of Brady's living room sofa. A thick, fuzzy blanket wraps my body. For a moment, I inhale scents spilled coffee and hazelnut creamer—*Mom*—but reality hits, and the once comfortable aroma is replaced with asparagus and peanut butter.

Yuck!

Speaking of Mom, she never came home last night. Neither did Brady.

"Yoo-hoo, Candy! Time to wake up!" Laurell's voice rings my ear, and I squint at her pinched-lip expression.

She wears a black tracksuit with her hair in a bun. Swimming goggles hang around her neck. I can't decide what's more alarming—Laurell breaking into the apartment or Laurell doing so at 5:30 a.m.

That means I'm operating with only three hours of sleep.

I yawn noisily.

"Oh, yuck!" Laurell waves her hand in front of her face. "You may look like Sleeping Beauty, but you have the breath of an ogre!"

"What are you doing here?" I push myself up. I struggle to believe that Laurell is here, but after the elves, I can almost believe anything.

"You were taking forever, so my mom sent me up. Good thing she did. You would have slept through practice," Laurell says, twirling a set of keys on her fingers. If we're best friends in the Cursed World, then she probably has a spare key. Maggie does for Mom's apartment in the Normal World. One mystery solved.

"Practice for what?" I scrub crusties from my eye.

"Swim practice, of course!"

I groan and drop back onto the couch. Of all the lies that came true, why did it have to be the one I told Laurell at the beach BBQ? Seriously, it's just as minor as the excuse I gave Mom about my room.

"The elves!" I cry, launching from the sofa.

"Elves?" Laurell repeats with confusion.

I ignore her and stop in front of my bedroom. Pressing my ear against the door, I listen for any sort of noise. The room is silent.

I let out a relieved breath. Turning the door handle, I let myself inside. The once stunning birthday cake room looks more like a cake someone dropped to the floor.

"Your room!" Laurell cries, following me. "What happened? Were you robbed?"

"You wouldn't believe me if I told you," I mutter. I step on chewed bubblegum and wince.

Laurell points to the closet. "Why do you have your dresser there? Please don't tell me you're, like, hiding a body in there."

"Eight bodies," I say, and Laurell looks at me like I've lost my mind. "Eight six-inch bodies that destroyed my room. They're alive, at least."

"I'll be waiting with my mom in the car." She carefully backtracks over the broken trophies. "Seriously, clean your room when you get the chance. No pedicure nights at your place until you do."

"Right," I agree, only to get her out of my space.

When I know for sure that Laurell has left the apartment, I creep toward the closet. My shaky breaths fill the silence. Leaning over the dresser, I hear faint snoring.

Curiosity is tempting, and I debate moving the dresser just a smidge to sneak a peek at the elves.

Don't, I tell myself as my instincts kick in. I take a cautious step backward. If I let the elves loose, I can't imagine the type of revenge they'd invoke on me for locking them in the closet. Plus, I might cry at the sight of my perfect closet ruined.

I bend down and lift a pink, flowery maxi dress off of the floor. Pieces of torn schoolwork stick to the soft fabric. I gently wipe them away. At least I have a few outfits scattered on the ground to choose from.

My phone vibrates. Laurell and her mom are waiting. Sighing, I rub my hand down my face and debate a way to avoid going to swim practice. Waiting for them to leave won't work. Laurell will just come back up here and drag me downstairs. Coming up with an excuse won't work, thanks to Mrs. Gulligan.

Except . . . I haven't tried texting a lie.

Does the curse affect written lies?

Only one way to find out.

Grabbing my phone, I send the text. *I'm not feeling too good. I don't think I should go to practice.*

I wait for the Delivered notification.

Failed.

A bad feeling brews in my stomach. I try to send the text again, only to receive the same status. A third time proves fruitless, as well.

My phone has full bars, so it's not the service provider or a poor connection.

I try another tactic—honesty.

Getting dressed. Almost ready. This time when I hit send, the text goes through without a problem.

Not a moment later, Laurell responds. *Hurry!*

I guess this means I don't have a choice.

Frowning, I slowly lower my phone. I swear I smell the faintest wisps of black licorice and realization hits. In the Cursed World, I cannot lie. Not with words, not with texts, and probably not with any other method. I've lost the one thing that made me, *me*.

Who is Candy Sky if she cannot lie?

***

My sneakers squish into the soggy mat in the Neiwood Recreation Center locker room. The air is thick with chlorine and shampoo. Voices ping-pong off the teal tiled walls, and I wince at the loud sound of a toilet flushing.

Laurell leads me to one of the changing rooms where the girls our age—some I recognize from school—and a few high schoolers are dressing in matching tie-dye swimsuits. When they finish tucking their hair into rubber caps, they disappear down a hallway toward the pool.

We stop at two empty lockers. Laurell drops her duffle bag on a bench and digs out her swimwear, a replica to what everyone else is wearing. The word "tsunami" is displayed in bulky letters on the chest, shaped to resemble a wave.

I stand awkwardly behind Laurell, rubbing my wrist and staring at the floor as she strips out of her street clothes. She glances at me and does a double take at the sight of my maxi dress soaking at the hem.

"Did you forget your swim gear?" she asks.

"Y-Yeah, I guess," I swallow thickly.

Laurell wiggles her head through the straps of her goggles and drapes them across her neck.

"Better go ask Coach for one of his backups," she says. "Hopefully he remembered to wash them. Last time someone borrowed a suit, it was still wet and smelled of mold."

I scrunch my nose.

"Where is the coach?" I tug on my dress. The slimy fabric trails against my calves, sending shivers up my body.

"Where do you think?" She puckers her lips at the mirror in her locker. "By the pool, duh."

"Right." I remain frozen in place. Every fiber of my being tells me to fake sickness and leave. I can't swim laps. I can barely dog paddle. Even then, I only try when Maggie is nearby, ready to rescue me if I start to drown.

Maybe in the Cursed World, I know how to swim? What if my body recognizes the different strokes, even if my mind does not? Should I test my luck?

Laurell slips an arm through mine before I make my decision. "Better not waste any more time. You know how the couch gets when someone is late. Extra laps for everyone," she groans.

The hallway to the pool reminds me of the vacuum hose Mom uses to seal her clothes into plastic bags. As we walk, the walls narrow and elongate. The sight of the lap lanes through the glass door steals the air from my lungs.

The pool room is uncomfortably warm. A large group of students gather at the shallow end of the pool, all waiting in swimsuits and trunks. I'm the odd one out.

On the opposite end, a man in a red polo-shirt flips through papers on his clipboard. A metal whistle dangles on his chest. He must be the coach. Laurell confirms my suspicions when she leads me toward him. I jolt to a stop when I notice the boy standing next to him.

Sayer Lafayette.

He wears a t-shirt that matches the team swimwear, holding a clipboard like the coach. I recall our earlier conversation. He is the only person who can tell the difference between the Cursed World and the Normal World.

I curl my shoulders forward and duck my head as we approach. Sayer's eyebrows raise. I feel exposed. He's the only one who knows about Mrs. Gulligan, so it's safe to say he will notice the differences in the Cursed World–like how I'm not actually on the swimming team. I just hope he won't make a scene. I'm too exhausted for any more drama, especially after dealing with the elves.

"Candy!" the coach booms. "How's our favorite sailfish?"

Favorite sailfish? What kind of nickname is that?

"She forgot her gear," Laurell answers.

The coach raises an eyebrow, and I force an apologetic smile.

"It must have slipped my mind," I chuckle awkwardly, ignoring Sayer's gobsmacked expression.

The coach jabs his thumb at a black duffle bag propped against the lifeguard stand. "Take a cap and some goggles, too," he says.

Gulping nervously, I shuffle over to the bag. I find something that fits me almost immediately. I hold it up to my body and feel my stomach sink.

"Hit the locker room. We're about to start our warmups." The coach gently taps his clipboard on top of my head.

"Don't suppose you have a towel," I ask meekly, and he points to a shelf of white towels next to an industrial hamper.

"Forgetting your gear is so unlike you," he says.

"Sorry."

The coach grins widely at me. "Don't worry about it! We all have our off days, even you. Our state champion!"

Sayer's clipboard clatters to the ground.

"What!" he shouts, and I cringe.

"Did I say something wrong?" The coach's head swivels between the two of us.

"She's not the state champion." Sayer looks me up and down, nose scrunching as though he smells something sour. "She's not even on the team."

My breath catches in my throat. I bite my lip as the coach crosses his arms and gives Sayer a hard look.

"Have you lost your mind or something?" the coach asks. "Or is this a social media prank?"

"I'll prove it to you." Sayer retrieves his fallen clipboard. "She's never been on the attendance list." He trails a finger down a roster of swimmers, murmuring my full name under his breath. He stops and blinks in astonishment. "No way," he whispers. "It can't be."

"Enough fooling around. You were there for the state championships. You watched her place first."

"No, I watched Brittany Pearl place first," Sayer argues.

"Are you in on this?" The coach turns to me.

"I . . . well, no," I stutter. "I mean, he's right. I'm not the state champion."

"You've both been drinking too much pool water," the coach says, waving me off. "Go change."

"But—"

Ignoring me, he faces the water, lifts his whistle, and blows hard. The chatter around the pool ceases. Without being told, all of the swimmers form lines in front of each lane.

"Warm up!" the couch bellows, and the first swimmer of each lane jumps into the pool. "Medley!"

Clutching the swimsuit and goggles to my chest, I realize I have no choice. I turn away from Sayer's burning gaze and slog robotically back to the locker room.

I'm alone when I enter the dank changing room. The moisture on the tiled walls creates distorted reflections of me as I pass. The ominous vibe gives me second thoughts, and I hurry to a private changing stall, unsettled. I stare at the swimsuit in my hand. Why have I let myself get this far?

I should have faked sickness, with or without words, the moment Laurell mentioned swim practice back at Brady's apartment.

What is stopping me from walking out of here right now? Laurell isn't around to pressure me. I can leave the borrowed swimsuit by her locker, and she can return it to the coach.

I catch sight of myself in the mirror, framed by the Picasso versions of my face reflecting on the tiled walls. I am everything I have ever wanted to be. I have perfect designer clothes, perfect grades, and the perfect boyfriend.

I guess I just have to see if this new world came with swimming powers. I suppose I could tell the truth, but that's absurd. Candy Sky tell the truth? Ha! The day that happens is the day I give up Elijah Nole—never.

I blow a loose strand of hair from my face, giving myself a determined nod. *You got this.*

***

I shiver as I join the swimmers. Half of them are dripping wet, huffing from exertion, and crossing their arms for warmth. The other half are waiting for their turn at warmups. I spot Laurell. She is still dry. I cut through the lines and stand next to her.

My eyes never leave the swimmers in the water. I try to memorize their movements. Unfortunately, not everyone is doing the same stroke. Some of the swimmers propel through the water like dolphins, their arms moving in symmetrical circles. Others swim like frogs. I recognize both freestyle and backstroke.

Which stroke am I supposed to do?

"What are you doing in our line?" Laurell leans over and whispers.

I blink, glancing away from the pool. "What do you mean?"

"Your line is over there," she points to a cluster of towering behemoths—the high schoolers. "Hurry, before Coach Padilla thinks we're fooling around. He'll assign us extra laps."

"Seriously?" I squawk.

Laurell stares at me as though I've grown two heads. She shoos me away, and I begrudgingly switch lanes.

Hugging my shaky frame, I'm tempted to ask the girl ahead of me which stroke I should do. Judging by her well-developed body, though, she is at least sixteen. The age difference intimidates me. I've never spoken to a high schooler before.

The line moves with the sharp tweet of the coach's whistle. By the time the girl ahead of me jumps into the water and kicks off the wall, tremors wrack my entire body. I step back and bump into a wet, cold torso, trapping me from escaping.

The swimmers reach the other end of the pool. They flip in the water and head back. The coach blows his whistle.

"Next!" he shouts.

I go rigid. Bile rises in my throat. Someone nudges me from behind when I stand there for too long. I plug my nose and jump in.

Cold water electrifies my limbs. I break through the surface and gasp, standing with most of my body out of the water. "Cold, cold, cold!" The chant rattles through the chattering of my teeth. Several swimmers chuckle.

"Come on, Candy! Get swimming!" the coach calls.

I'm the only one still clinging to the wall, and I flush when almost everyone turns to watch me. Taking a deep breath, I plunge back into the water, maneuvering my legs until they are crouched against the pool's wall, and spring forward.

As I propel down the lane, astonishingly making it halfway before I need to take a breath, the best-case scenario happens: My body takes control and soon I'm cruising down the lane like a seasoned Olympic swimmer. My movements? Flawless. Timing? Perfect. My lungs act as though this is a simple stroll in the park. In fact, I can almost hear my lungs saying, "C'mon, Candy! What else have you got? This is for kindergarteners."

Just kidding.

I wish that happened. It's too bad I can't even lie to myself.

After I propel down the lane, making it a pathetic two or three feet before I need to take a breath, the worst-case scenario happens: My body does not take control, and soon I'm flailing and bobbing like a head of cauliflower. Water floods my goggles until I have no choice but to close my eyes. Fear of drowning replaces my initial worry of embarrassing myself.

What was I thinking? Me? A champion swimmer? I can't even climb a flight of stairs without nearly keeling over at the top. My sport is flipping through designer catalogs.

Enough is enough. I do what I know best—doggy paddle.

I ignore my rising mortification. All I can hear is water splashing and wheezing breaths, but my brain fabricates mocking laughter. *Just get to the other side,* I urge myself. Then, I can call it quits and hide in one of the bathroom stalls until everyone is old and wrinkly and has forgotten about Candy Sky.

At some point, my toes no longer touch the bottom of the pool. I gulp water painfully, struggling to stay afloat. I have no choice but to twist around and float on my back. This gives me a moment of rest.

A very brief moment.

"Butterfly, Candy!" I hear the coach yell, despite my submerged ears.

If giving him the middle finger didn't mean I'd lose the battle to stay afloat, then he would be benching me for the rest of practice. Possibly, he might call my parents.

Gathering what dignity I have left, I flip over to float on my back. Pain lances up my thigh. A Charlie horse! The muscle jerks and coils, a snake slithering under my skin. I imagine this is how being stabbed feels like.

I scream.

Or try to.

Water gushes into my mouth, filling my lungs. I try to keep my head above the surface, but the pool seems to morph into a treacherous sea. Violent waves and strong currents pull me under. Throat constricting. Eyes glazing. My mind is a dandelion seed detaching itself from the stem and drifting away in the wind. I stare at the kaleidoscope of ceiling lights as I drown for the second time.

TWELVE
Cursed

When I break the surface of the water, a muscled arm hauls me onto solid ground. Someone whacks my back hard, helping expel water from my lungs. I cough until I puke. Flopping on my side, I close my eyes and breathe.

Am I really alive?

There are voices all around, but I can't make sense of what they are saying over the ringing in my ears. A towel is draped over me.

Eventually, I squint through my lashes at a mop of drenched curly brown hair. Sayer Lafayette is on the ground next to me, clothes soaked. He rests a hand on my back, and I realize he is the one who saved me.

A crowd gathers, but the coach quickly barks for everyone to wait on the other side of the pool. The numbness in my head disperses into conscious thought. I sob. Tears and snot drip down my face. I almost drowned.

Again.

I push myself up, and the coach grasps my arms, helping me to my feet.

"Let's go see the nurse," he says, wrapping another towel around my shoulders.

I barely register the walk to the recreation center's offices. One minute, I'm getting stares from worried teammates, and then the next I'm ushered onto a medical cot. The coach explains the incident to the nurse, and she replaces my damp towel with a thick wool blanket. They are already on the phone, calling Mom.

After a moment, the coach clicks his tongue and glares at his phone. "Voicemail," he grumbles. He tries again. No answer.

"How typical," he says. "Let's go see who's on your emergency contact list."

My heart stutters. Not Brady! Anyone but him! He's still a stranger and a product of Mrs. Gulligan's lie. After the elves and nearly drowning in the pool, I'm starting to question if the curse does have major pitfalls, after all. The coach leaves the room before I voice my wishes. I'm left to answer the nurse's onslaught of questions.

The door to the nurse's office opens, and Sayer comes inside. Water drips from his clothes, despite the towel wrapped around him. His hair has been rubbed partially dry, his damp curls slowly standing up again.

The nurse asks if Sayer is hurt, but he shakes his head. He asks for extra clothes, and the nurse begins rummaging through drawers by her desk.

She finds a white t-shirt and some basketball shorts. Sayer uses the restroom to change. When he emerges, he returns to the seat by the bed.

"Coach wants me to sit with you," Sayer says, noticing my confusion.

"Ah," I respond gravely. My throat feels scratchy from all the coughing.

Sayer folds his fingers together and leans forward. He eyes the nurse as she fills out an incident report.

"Before yesterday, I had barely heard your name in the rumor mill at school," he whispers. "Then, out of nowhere, everyone knows you and acts like you have done all these amazing things." Sayer pauses, the corner of his lip twitching before lifting into a grim smile. "What did you do to anger Mrs. Gulligan?"

"So it's true," I whisper. "You are the only person who hasn't changed in the Cursed World."

"I'm guessing there's more to all this than instant popularity and you becoming a swim team champion?"

I nod.

"I created a list. I can show you after I get my bag from the locker room." Although, I need to update the list before I show Sayer. A lot has happened since buying the DSC dress. "My best friend Maggie always warned me that Mrs. Gulligan was a witch. I thought she was just trying to keep me from getting on Mrs. Gulligan's bad side. Who would have thought the rumors were true!"

"You still haven't told me what you did," Sayer says.

Flinching, I turn away so that Sayer doesn't see my shame. I don't want to admit that lying put me in this situation. I can already hear Maggie's big, fat "I told you so."

I wish she was here to tell me what to do.

"Well?" Sayer pushes. "Are you going to tell me?"

"Maybe later," I mumble.

"How can I help you break the curse if I don't know what it is?" Sayer asks.

"You want to help me?" I blink. "Why?"

Sayer drops his gaze to his hands. They clench until his knuckles turn a chalky brown.

"For the longest time, I thought I was the only one. I almost convinced myself that the curse was a dream just so I didn't go crazy. Aside from discovering that someone is going through the same thing as me, I never broke my—"

The office door slams open, interrupting our conversation. Yolanda barges inside. She appears at my side in an instant and throws her arms around me. I squeak as she pulls me into a bone-crushing hug. Over her shoulder, I watch Sayer raise a brow.

"I came as soon as your coach called," Yolanda says. "Thank goodness I was in town!"

My heart thuds painfully. Mom really couldn't make it? Her daughter almost drowned! If that doesn't spur her into making an appearance, I don't know what will.

As much as I like Yolanda, I want Mom to tuck me under a blanket on the couch and comfort me with soft jazz and a cup of coffee.

"Shall we get going?" Yolanda asks.

"I have to pick up my things from the locker room," I say.

"Lead the way." Yolanda helps me to my feet. Her hand rests on my neck.

Before we leave the room, Sayer calls out.

"Meet me in the library during lunch? If not, after school?"

I take a deep breath, emotions tugging in all sorts of directions. I'm not sure that I want to meet with Sayer and work on breaking my curse. Sure, a few bad things have happened, but that hardly compares to the good, right?

I need food and sleep before I can think about this any further.

"Maybe," I whisper.

***

Yolanda heads toward a local cafe after my stomach growls for the fifteenth time. Driving through the heart of Neiwood, we pass the road that leads to the Calico Oyster. I open my mouth, about to demand we go there for breakfast leftovers, but then recall the lie I told Mrs. Gulligan. The Calico Oyster most likely doesn't exist in the Cursed World.

Dejected, I slouch in my seat.

The mom-n-pop cafe is one that Mom takes me to sometimes. The outside is brick with a classic red-and-white awning. Through the windows, I spot people sipping espresso and eating pastries. A display case at the end of the dining room holds a mix of sweet and savory breakfast items.

The street is packed, so we park a block away and walk. On a normal day, the distance wouldn't bother me. However, after swim practice, reaching the cafe entrance and making it to my seat feels like a marathon. Thankfully, Yolanda orders food from the counter for us. I battle dozing off for a few minutes before she returns with massive cinnamon rolls that are smothered in hot, gooey frosting.

This is exactly what I need to turn my day around.

I jab my fork into the cinnamon roll and tear off large chunks, taking a ginormous bite. Yolanda is a bit more graceful, using a knife to cut hers, but soon we both have globs of melted frosting at the corners of our mouths.

Yolanda dabs her face with a napkin, only for it to stick to her face. I snort a laugh through another bite.

My mood lightens.

"I'm in town for the week," Yolanda says.

"Really?" I perk at the news.

"With the talk show, I won't be around as often." She takes a sip of her cappuccino. "I want to make sure you have enough supportive people in your life. I hate seeing you all alone."

I flinch.

"I have Maggie," I insist. Deep down, though, I know something is off about my best friend in the Cursed World. It's almost like Maggie doesn't exist.

I hope I'm wrong.

"Who?" Yolanda tilts her head.

"A best friend who supports me," I quickly correct.

"I've never met Maggie. Now Laurell, on the other hand . . ." Yolanda huffs, rolling her eyes.

"You don't like her?" I blink with surprise.

"Don't act like Laurell is innocent," she says. "You know what trouble she got you both into last school year."

My fork stops inches from my mouth, and I glance up at Yolanda. Her face looks like she licked a lemon.

"What trouble?" I ask, mind flickering to the rumors of Laurell switching out Beth Abbot's hand cream. I push the thought away, though. No one could prove she did it. Plus, in the Cursed World, she seems perfectly nice.

"Let's not talk about this here." Yolanda thumps her coffee down with finality.

She can't just say something like that and expect me to not have questions! Why bring something up if we're not going to talk about it? What kind of trouble did Laurell and I get into? How severe did it have to be for Yolanda to seem so uneasy now?

A ping breaks my thoughts. I check my phone.

Laurell told me about swim practice. Are you okay?

Oh. My. Gosh. Elijah Nole texted me. Me. I know that I'm his girlfriend in the Cursed World, but I haven't heard from him since I got here. I was beginning to worry. Something good did come from almost drowning!

I grin so hard my cheeks hurt, texting him back. *I'm fine now. My cousin is stealing me from school for the day.*

Mostly to recover but also to hang out.

His response is immediate. *Yolanda?*

Yep!

My phone chirps again. *You promised I could meet her . . . . Want to join me for lunch?*

Breath escapes my lungs. I bite my lower lip, hopeful. *Of course I want to. I should ask Yolanda first. Where at?*

Yolanda looks up as I receive another text. *I was invited by someone from the recording studio for lunch on a yacht. You should come. It's kinda an all-afternoon thing, though. Make sure Yolanda knows when you ask.*

"You seem pleased," Yolanda winks. "A boy?"

"Elijah Nole," I admit bashfully.

"The pop singer?" Yolanda raises her brow.

"Yeah, we started going out last week. He invited us onto a yacht for the afternoon." I lick my lips and look at Yolanda with begging eyes. "Can we go? I'm dying to see him. He was taken out of school this week for recording. Plus, he wants to meet you."

"Hmmm." Yolanda twirls her hair in thought. "I admit this is a great networking opportunity, especially for the talk show."

"Does this mean we can go?" I barely breathe.

Yolanda smiles. "Let's buy new outfits for the trip," she says.

Cursed World

- I live in a super nice apartment with a man named Brady.
- I have a dream room and a dream closet.
- I'm ~~friends~~ best friends with Laurell.
- I have a famous cousin named Yolanda Nox.
- I'm a straight -A student.
- ELIJAH NOLE IS MY BOYFRIEND!
- ELIJAH NOLE IS MY BOYFRIEND!
- ELIJAH NOLE IS MY BOYFRIEND!
  This totally deserved three bullet points.
- I'M GOING TO THE DANCE WITH ELIJAH NOLE!
- Mrs. Gulligan does not exist.
- I'm a frequent shopper at David Silk Collection.
- I have a credit card!
- Elves attacked me. Elves! They exist!
- I'm a champion swimmer . . . not really.
- Maggie is MIA.

THIRTEEN
A Fishing Trip To Remember

The wooden docks of the marina creak under our feet. Around fifty or sixty yachts are tied to the five available docks, with the larger cruise-type boats and charters harboring the furthest one. A speed boat carefully pulls into the fuel station at the end of Dock 5, where two attendants wait with a gas hose. The sight of the water causes the hairs on my arm to rise. I must not be over nearly drowning.

Twice.

The sky has darkened to a sooty gray, and mist threatens to rain. I wrap my arms around myself and shiver. My breaths form white puffs. When did the temperature plummet? The forecast said today would be in the low seventies, but the air is frigid and wintry.

Yolanda said the sea can be brisk, but I wasn't expecting this.

I'm grateful that Yolanda insisted I purchase a denim jacket to go over my new black and white sailor dress. I'm also glad she talked me out of the pumps, pushing me toward the white flats instead. I imagine the heels catching in the cracks between the planks and me falling into the brackish water.

I'm done playing fish for the rest of the year.

"Colder than usual for California." Yolanda reads my mind.

"It's still technically summer!" I agree.

Yolanda raises her marina map. Slip 6 on Dock 5 is circled in dark ink. The marina manager was kind enough to mark where we're supposed to go. By the looks of it, we are heading toward the larger yachts and charters.

"Luckily, the waves don't look too rough. Otherwise, we might need to reschedule this,"

Yolanda says. "Then again, I'm no boating expert."

Seagulls squawk from the dock covering. Barnacles climb the log support beams, and in the water below us, schools of fish swim in circles. The air grows colder with each passing second, and I swear a snow flurry tumbles past my face.

But that's impossible. Neiwood only sees snow in the middle of winter. This is definitely the result of a lie. But which one? I wrack my brain, but I come up blank.

We turn onto the last dock of the marina, and I spot Elijah immediately, fiddling with a line in front of a massive luxury yacht. Along with his incognito cap and sunglasses, he wears a flannel shirt and plain jeans. I hardly recognize him as the vibrant pop singer.

Smiling widely, I break into a run. I call out his name, waving my arm feverishly over my head. All of my problems from the last twenty-four hours disappear as I skid to a stop next to my crush. No—my *boyfriend*.

"Elijah! Oh. Em. Gee. I'm so excited you invited us!" I squeal.

"Yeah, sure–whatever," Elijah says rather dismissively. He stares over my shoulder. "Is that Yolanda?"

My chest deflates. I had expected some enthusiasm. Maybe a hug?

"In the flesh," I say, hiding my hurt.

We've only been going out for a week, I remind myself. Calm down. We probably haven't even reached the holding hands phase.

Yolanda reaches my side, beaming brightly. "Elijah Nole! I've heard so much about you, and not from the media." She winks at me.

I duck my head, peeking through my bangs at Elijah's perfect face. He looks even cuter in person than he does on TV. I sigh dreamily.

"Find this place okay?" he asks Yolanda.

"Yes, we did, thank you," she smiles. "And thank you for inviting us. Lunch on the water sounds lovely."

"You got here just in time. We're planning on heading out in about ten minutes."

Elijah leads us to the back of the boat. He takes Yolanda's purse as she climbs aboard. I watch as she climbs the stairs to the deck. I'm eager to join her, but my legs lock at the gap I must cross between the boat and the dock.

I gulp at the sight of the waves.

"What's the matter? Why aren't you climbing inside?" Elijah asks.

"Sorry, the water is freaking me out a bit." I rub my arm self-consciously.

"You're about to be around a lot of water."

I frown at his tone. Does he not remember that I almost drowned this morning? Can't the Cursed World cut me a little break? Does *everything* have to involve water?

Elijah sighs, and he holds out a hand. "Here, let me help you."

I stare at his palm, mouth suddenly dry. My heartbeat quickens as I lift my hand to take his. I forget about the ocean below, and I blush as Elijah helps me aboard.

I feel like the luckiest girl on Earth for having such a thoughtful boyfriend—a thoughtful, talented, and famous boyfriend.

Elijah follows me up the stairs, and at the top, I gawk at the wood-planked deck. Curved patio sofas sit around a centered fireplace, navy blue throw pillows contrasting with the furniture's white fabric.

"Welcome!" booms a man with a heavy Texas accent. He steps out of a door leading to the cabin.

He strides toward us, leather boots clopping against the ground. A brown Stenson shades his face-splitting smile. The man reminds me of a stereotypical cowboy!

"The name's Van," he says, shaking Yolanda's hand before taking mine. "Glad to have lunch with such lovely ladies."

"He's from the recording studio," Elijah says. "He owns the yacht."

"I'd serve lunch on the deck, but this weather has me questioning whether I'm in California or Antarctica." The real-life cowboy bellows whoopee.

Footsteps sound from the stairs. A tall, slender man in a dress shirt and slacks appears behind us. His dark hair and beard are neatly trimmed, and he has stern blue eyes. He carries a plastic bag of goods from the marina store.

He regards Yolanda.

"I'm Dean Reynolds, Elijah's manager."

"And uncle," Elijah chimes in.

"Pleasure to meet you." Yolanda's tone is business-like. I have a feeling they will be talking privately at some point today about possibly covering Elijah on Yolanda's talk show. Why else would Elijah insist on meeting her?

After another round of formal greetings, Dean turns his attention to me. "Nice to see you again, Candy."

I blink dumbly for a moment. He knows Candy of the Cursed World. How?

Reynolds. His last name sounds so familiar. And he is Elijah's uncle. My eyes widen as the dots connect. He is Laurell's dad!

Of course Candy of the Cursed World knows him. She practically grew up with Laurell and her family judging by the photo album I found. I wonder how many more strangers know me on a personal level.

"Let's get y'all warmed up in the cabin," Van beckons for us to follow.

I inhale sharply as we enter the cabin. A white-leather sectional takes up the entirety of one wall, and across from it is a bar with matching leather stools and the largest wall-mounted television I have ever seen. In front of the sofa, a table is set with iridescent black dishware and a bronze kraken centerpiece. The walls are mostly window glass, ensuring a complete view of the bay and marina. At the bow, touch-screen control panels, three reclining chairs, and a powered steering wheel make up the captain's controls. Next to the panels is a narrow door labeled Engine and Radio Room.

"Kick off your shoes and store them over there," Van says, pointing to a shoe rack. "The fridge is stocked with drinks, and there's appetizers already on warming plates on the counter. There are jalapeno poppers, bacon wrapped smokies, and caprese salad—help yourself. Once we get out on sea, I'll fire up the grill and cook us some oysters and a couple of sea bass I caught before recording this morning."

I slip off my shoes and walk further into the room, drinking in its sheer luxury. I plop down on the sofa and spread my arms out. Yolanda takes full advantage of the food and plucks a jalapeno popper by the toothpick, moaning as she eats it in one bite. From the short time I've known her, I can tell that Yolanda is a big foodie. She takes one more of the pepper, before she shuffles over to the bacon-wrapped weenies.

Elijah disappears down a hallway next to the entrance of the cabin, which I assume leads to the bedrooms, and returns with a Nintendo Switch. He sits on the cushion next to me, not close enough for physical contact. Still, I feel the dip in the couch as he sinks into the leather, and that's enough for me.

Van and Dean prepare the boat for departure. Soon, the boat shudders to life, and the marina disappears behind us. There's something so surreal about this moment. Here I am, sitting next to Elijah Nole. I'm on the fanciest boat I've ever seen, embarking on an adventure with strangers. Still, all I can think about is how I never got Mom's approval for this.

In the Normal World, Mom would have had a stroke if she learned I did this without talking to her first. I guess Mom of the Cursed World really doesn't care. I mean, I almost drowned this morning and neither Yolanda nor I have received a text or phone call from her. It's unbelievable!

I watch the boat glide toward the mouth of Morgan Bay, passing by the beach where Maggie and I always paddle board, and then where the natural bridge to the abandoned lighthouse is submerged under the high tide. Once outside the bay, Van, who sits in the captain's chair, kicks the speed up a notch, and the boat soon zips over the water, bouncing off the waves.

I shift so that I lean over the sofa, pressing my face against the window. The ocean lacks its usual glittery beauty. Instead, it's black and intimidating with barely any light to reflect the overcast sky. The flurries are now fat snowflakes.

"I've never seen anything like this," I overhear Dean say. "Maybe we should cancel."

"Shoulda made that call while we were docked," Van says.

"It's not too late to turn back," says Laurell's dad.

"Relax, will ya? The sea is calm, and the wind is only 12 knots."

"Mixing cold air and warm waters is a bad combination. Plus, it's difficult to see the coast."

Dean isn't wrong. A fog has settled on the water, shrouding the mainland. Looking out the window, I can no longer tell if I'm facing North or South or any other direction. My stomach quivers with butterflies.

Again, something about this situation seems so familiar, but I can't place it.

Van pulls a lever, and the boat slows to a much more comfortable speed.

"If the storm gets worse, we'll turn back. We're almost to where I want to take y'all," Van promises.

Worried, I lower myself from the window and contemplate how to distract myself. Yolanda has joined the front of the boat, taking the chair on the other side of Van. I'm left with Elijah, which isn't a bad thing.

If anything, this is the perfect time to talk!

"Now, about the dance this Friday," I begin, snagging a throw pillow from beside me. I need something to hug and keep me grounded after everything that's happened. "I got your invite. Obviously, I'll go with you! I already bought my dress. Do you want to know what colors it is? We can find you something that matches."

Elijah moves the joysticks of his Switch, completely enthralled by his game.

I don't think he heard me.

"Elijah," I singsong.

He still doesn't respond.

How rude! I harrumph.

The dance is days away, and we still haven't figured out any of the details. What time are we going to meet? Are we riding together or separately? Do we want to have dinner before the dance? If so, where?

I call out his name one more time before losing my patience. I reach out and snap my fingers in front of his face.

"Earth to Elijah!" I exclaim. "Do you have cotton in your ears?"

He sucks in an annoyed breath and drops his head back. "I died," he moans.

"I've been talking to you." I cross my arms.

"Go ahead. What is it?" He takes a sip from his orange juice.

I scoff. He acts like I'm an annoying sibling, not a girlfriend.

"About the dance, I want to know—"

The boat jolts violently, and I scream. Both Elijah and I fall out of our seats. Glass shatters around us. An ear-splitting scraping slides along the side of the boat before I hear crunching metal. An alarm blares from the captain's controls.

The air becomes stagnant with that horrible black licorice stench, and I pull the collar of my dress over my nose. Mrs. Gulligan's curse is at work.

A grating whine pierces the air from below the boat. Yolanda races into the cabin with the two men in tow. Van heads straight for the engine room, while Dean takes a seat at the captain's controls. He snatches a radio, a coiling cord connecting to the controls, and speaks into the receiver with barely concealed panic.

"Mayday, mayday, mayday! This is Bloody Mary, Bloody Mary, Bloody Mary. CA 828. Mayday, this is Bloody Mary." He spits out a long series of numbers that I can't keep up with. I do pick out two words--latitude and longitude. He's giving our location. "We're stuck on an unidentified object. Propeller failure and possible medical assistance. Three adults, two minors onboard. Bloody Mary is an eighty-foot cabin cruiser with white hull and white deck house. Over."

My stomach plummets, and I feel my whole body ignite with adrenaline.

The boat struck something, and I think I know what it was . . . .

Yolanda appears between me and Elijah. She grabs both of our arms and lifts us to our feet. She hauls us out of the cabin and onto the deck, thrusting life vests into our hands.

Snow plummets in sheets. The fog limits our visibility to only a few feet, and the bow disappears into a void of white. The wind nips with frost, and my knees quake together from the cold. Waves crash and rock the boat.

"Are we sinking?" Elijah asks, voice cracking from fear.

"I'm not sure." Yolanda gestures at the life vests and urges us to put them on.

When I clip the buckles together, Yolanda tightens the straps until it's snug. She does the same for Elijah.

Dean appears from the cabin, and he rushes over to the stern of the boat. Gripping the railing, he holds himself over the water to see the damage better. He clicks his tongue, before he lowers himself back onto the deck. Turning toward us, he frowns grimly.

"What happened?" Yolanda demands.

"You're not going to believe this" –he runs his fingers through his hair— "but we hit an iceberg."

Revelation strikes me like lightning, and my lungs constrict. I try breathing deeply to calm myself, but I choke on the reeking odor that follows me whenever magic is at play.

"We hit an iceberg!" Elijah smacks his head. "But we're in California!"

"Maybe it broke off from the Arctic?" I reason, though I know very well where the floating chunk of ice came from.

"It would have melted long before it hit the bottom of Alaska," Dean says. "This is one for the record book."

This is all because of Mrs. Gulligan! Frustrated, I grip my hair and pull.

"Van says there's no leaking," Dean says, leaning against the deck railing. "Looks like it's just a broken propeller. I radioed for help, but no one can make it to us until the storm passes. The coast guard has been contacted."

"That could be all night!" I remember the detail I told Mrs. Gulligan to explain why I scored a thirty percent on a test.

"We have enough food and supplies to last a week, even two, at sea," Dean assures.

"What should we do until we're rescued?" Yolanda asks.

"Don't panic, that's for sure. Keep a life jacket near you at all times," he says.

My breath comes out fast and panicked. Yolanda places a hand on my shoulder, but I shake her off and step away. She's a product of Mrs. Gulligan's magic. How do I know she won't trick me or cause more chaos?

The Cursed World is not working out how I hoped. In fact, it's turning out to be dangerous—an actual curse, not a botched one. I don't know how much more of it I can take.

I need to give Sayer's suggestion some thought.

FOURTEEN
The Bitter Truth

Yolanda and Dean shoo us into the bedrooms while they clean up all the glass in the cabin. I follow Elijah into a four-person room that reminds me of my bedroom above the Calico Oyster, all bunk and no space. Elijah takes the top bunk by the only window and returns to his video game.

I pace in the little foot space available, wringing my hands and holding my breath whenever I hear a creak from the boat. Are we sinking now? Did Van miss a leak somewhere? I don't want to drown for the *third* time.

After a while, Yolanda appears with a plate of snacks in one hand and taps on her phone with her other. She clicks her tongue and mutters about how there's no cell service this far out on the water. I bite my lower lip and wait for any news she might have, but Yolanda just plops another jalapeno popper in her mouth before gesturing for me to take one.

"How can you eat at a time like this!" I shrill, pushing the plate back toward her.

"How can I not?" Yolanda's cheeks bulge. "These apps are to die for!"

She's acting like hitting an iceberg isn't a big deal. An iceberg sank the Titanic! We could very well have the same fate. She won't be stuffing her face with bacon-wrapped anything at the bottom of the ocean.

"And you!" I round on Elijah, slapping the bed to catch his attention. "You're just lying there playing video games! Why is no one but me freaking out?"

Elijah groans. "You heard the guys. The boat is fine other than the propellers."

"It's not just that!" I clamp my mouth shut, feeling abnormally irritated with Elijah. It's not just his lack of panic about our situation, but also his lack of emotion toward our lunch together. This entire time, Elijah has been ignoring me for his video game. He hasn't acted like a normal boyfriend should.

As much as I want to bring up this issue, I know now is not the time.

"Watch a movie or something. I think Van might have some books around here somewhere. You love reading," he says.

Maybe the Candy of the Cursed World does, but I sure don't. I only read fashion magazines and celebrity fanfiction. Other than that, reading is Maggie's area of expertise.

"Listen, Candy." Yolanda places her arm around my shoulder and pulls me into a half hug. "We're all scared, but we have to find ways to keep our mind clear. How do you cope with stressful things at home?"

"I-I . . ." The question is tricky. I've never been asked this before.

"Do you paint to express yourself? Write? Read books? Jog?" Yolanda presses.

Now that I think about it, I don't really have a way to release pent up emotions. I doubt scouring the web for the latest details about Elijah Nole counts. Usually, I let my feelings build until I act out. Sometimes, I lie when I want something to go a certain way. I'm not like Maggie. She knows exactly what she wants and who she wants to be.

"Think of some things to distract yourself." Yolanda releases her hold on me. "I'm not saying this is the right time to do some soul searching, but destroying yourself over something totally outside of your control won't help. The best you can do is focus on what you can control—yourself. Your actions. Acknowledge the circumstance, embrace your feelings, and choose the action that best puts you and those you care about in a better position." She pauses, letting me soak in her words.

For a moment, I don't think she's even talking about our current circumstances. It's like she peeled back my skull and read the story of my life. Does Yolanda know more than she lets on?

I realize after a moment of tense silence that Yolanda is waiting for me to say something.

"Way to go all phisiophical on me," I mutter.

Yolanda smiles and pats my cheek. "It's philosophical, deary."

I dislike the endearment. It reminds me of Mrs. Gulligan.

"Whatever." I take a deep breath. "I'll figure something out. Maybe there's a deck of cards or a board game?"

"I'll ask Van," she winks. "I'll call you when all the glass is picked up."

With a huff, I lie down on the bunk below Elijah. The weight of his body pushes part of the foam mattress through the wood planks. I want to strike up a conversation with him, but too many emotions grind inside of me, leaving my mind singed and my body exhausted. Yolanda's sage words only contribute to the mix. A normal person would have said something like "You're going to be fine" or "Let's go over what to do in the worst-case scenario."

Yet, Yolanda went above and beyond with her spiel on coping with life's lack of control. Maybe I do need to embrace my feelings. It almost felt like a message, possibly a hint on how to break the curse. Maybe Mrs. Gulligan wants me to find a hobby? That seems incredibly unlikely. I must be missing something. Or overthinking Yolanda's words. I'm definitely overthinking.

It's not long before we hear Yolanda holler from the main part of the cabin. I take a deep breath, count to three before I exhale, and then push myself to stand. Noticing Elijah hasn't moved, I rap the railing of the top bunk in case he is too preoccupied to listen. He shifts his head and looks down at me.

"Are you coming?" I ask.

"Naw, I'm fine here." He waves his hand lazily.

My shoulders slump. "But don't you want to spend time together?"

Elijah is making getting to know him extremely difficult with this whole I'm-a-typical-teen-boy-who-ignores-the-world-for-swords-and-leveling-up attitude. He's supposed to be the boy of my dreams! A gentleman!

"Not really."

The words are a slap to my face.

"W-Why?" I ask.

"Candy, no offense, but you're just another crazy fangirl," he says.

My throat constricts, and my stomach plummets. "Why did you ask me to the dance, then?" I ask.

"You're kidding me, right?" he says. "You're the one who made the deal."

"What deal?" I frown.

He sets his Switch aside and rolls over to face me. "Are you seriously going to act clueless? The deal was that if I pretend to be your boyfriend, you would introduce Yolanda to my manager."

Something inside me snaps, and I stagger to the lower bunk and sit down. I thought he and Candy from the Cursed World like-liked each other, but it turns out that I—*she*—bribed him

Movement from the top bunk breaks my inner turmoil, and Elijah noisily clops down the ladder, jumping to the ground with a thud as he skips the last step. He stands in front of me with his arms crossed.

"The invitation was part of the act. You don't actually think I would take you to the dance? You're weird! I caught you reading stories about me—fanfiction—and digging in the trash for a fork I used."

If I could crawl into a hole and die, I would. I've never been more mortified in my life. I cover my face with my hands and bite my lower lip, hoping the pain will distract me from the devastating heartbreak. It doesn't. Tears well in the corners of my eyes.

"And now that Yolanda and my manager have met, I don't have a reason to continue this deal," he says, and I flinch.

So, that's it then. We aren't really together, and we aren't really going to the dance. Now that Elijah got what he wanted, he's dumping me. Deep down, I knew that dating him was too good to be true, but I'd hoped we'd have some sort of connection—that all those hours spent pouring over magazines and articles and online forums would pay off.

I was wrong. Turns out, I'm the one who fell for the hook, line, and sinker.

This infuriates me.

Teeth clenching, I seethe, "Candy Sky does the fishing, not you!"

"What are you talking—"

Before he can finish, I snatch his beloved game console from the top bunk.

"Hey!" he cries.

Lifting the console above my head, I lob it at the wall. The controllers break on impact, and I hear a satisfying crack before the console clatters to the ground. My heart hammers in my chest from adrenaline, and I feel satisfied.

"My Switch!" Elijah drops to his knees and gathers the pieces up. He throws me a glare, getting up to leave. "Wait until Dean hears about this!" he yells over his shoulder.

I stare at the ground where Elijah once stood, the gravity of our conversation setting in. Tears finally trickle down my cheeks, and I gasp at the heartache. I can't believe Elijah duped me. I also can't believe he's such a jerkasaurus. Has Elijah Nole always been this way? He seemed nice when we first met, helping me up after accidentally hitting me in the face with a soccer ball. But I guess a few-second interaction isn't enough time to truly get to know someone. That and he caught me being a creepy fangirl, no doubt rubbing him the wrong way.

Overwhelmed with disappointment, I dive into a bunk bed pillow and sob.

***

The rescue boats arrive in the early hours of the morning. Blinding lights flash through the window and startle me from my light doze. Sleep doesn't come easily when you're stranded at sea and heartbroken. I hear a chugging noise and voices shouting, and the yacht which has held its breath since striking the iceberg comes to life.

Yolanda appears in the doorway and ushers Elijah and I out to the deck, life vests on and wrapped in blankets taken from the bunk room. Two boats drift next to the yacht, a tugboat and a steel Coast Guard vessel with orange trim.

The unusual, magical snowstorm tapered off around midnight, and the black clouds had opened up to millions upon millions of stars. Although the fog has lifted, the sea is nothing but darkness broken by the light emitting from the boats.

The coast guards help us climb onto their vessel, and we are ushered into a cabin where they ask us dozens of questions. Where are you from? Where were you born? What's your date of birth? Are you hurt anywhere? Do you require any kind of timed medication?

I'm so excited about going home that I don't mind the awkwardness of sitting next to Elijah. I grin when one of the coast guards mentions our parents waiting for us at the docks in Neiwood.

We wait for Dean to join us before the boat finally takes off. Van stays behind with his beloved yacht, which will be towed to a boat yard for repairs. I hope my lie-come-true hasn't caused too much damage.

I push down the guilt.

When we arrive at the Neiwood Marina, I spot a group of people huddled together by a nearby store. Two sets of reporters and camera operators mingle in front of an ambulance and a couple of police cars. Red hair catches my attention, and I sag with relief knowing Mom is amongst the people waiting for us, even if she is arm and arm with Brady.

The boat docks, and we are released to our families. Mom yanks me into a fierce hug that squeezes the air out of my lungs and causes the bones in my arms to creak. Brady gives me an awkward pat on the back, asking me if I'm okay. I close my eyes in the midst of Mom's hug and inhale her scent. I know she wouldn't smell like coffee since Mom of the Cursed World doesn't drink it, but I wasn't expecting peanut butter and asparagus to cling to her clothes. I cringe and turn my face away, taking in the crisp, wintery air.

"I'm so glad you're okay!" Mom says. I feel the wetness of her tears trickle through my hair. Mom loosens her hold enough to look me in the eye. "I am so, so sorry I missed Coach Padilla's calls this morning. I was just so busy at work." More tears drip down her face, and Mom lunges forward and peppers my face with kisses.

I jerk my head to the side, failing to dodge her puckered lips. Something is off about what she said. Didn't my lie include Mom losing her job? She became a party girl and was fired, and that's why she and Candy of the Cursed World moved in with Brady. Maybe I'm overthinking things, but the way she sobs dramatically, placing a hand against her forehead as though she's about to faint in relief, seems fake. It's like she's pretending to be a worried parent.

Too bad she sucks at acting.

Yolanda appears beside us. She offers Brady a firm, blank-faced handshake, and then she pulls Mom into a hug.

"Before you think I'm the worst babysitter in the world" –Yolanda brings her hands together— "just know there was no way to predict an iceberg in California."

"Babysitter?" I bristle at the word.

Yolanda winks at me. "Teen-sitter. Sorry. Your mom wanted me to keep an eye on you after swim practice this morning."

I whip my head toward Mom, and I watch her stiffen. "I thought you were at work and missed the calls."

"I was—I did," she stammers. "I was in a meeting, so I called Yolanda as soon as I could."

"A meeting at 6 a.m.? Right, like I believe that." I bark a laugh. "News flash, I know you lost your job."

"Candice," Mom says warningly.

"You just didn't want to be bothered by your daughter." My voice rises. "I almost drowned! You couldn't have taken a second to check in and see if I was okay?"

"Quiet, Candy. You're causing a scene," Brady says, stepping between me and my mother. His eyes remain on the reporters not too far from us. Of course, they're too preoccupied interviewing Elijah.

"I don't know what's worse," I continue, shaking my head, "you lying about missing Coach Padilla's calls or you lying that you actually care about me."

"Enough!" Brady says. "We can discuss this in the car. You better drop that attitude first, otherwise we're going to have some serious words."

I open my mouth to argue, but an EMT interrupts us. He insists on giving me a check-up in one of the ambulances, and I eagerly accept a break from Mom and her horrible boyfriend. I need some time to calm down and process my emotions.

As I follow him to the back of an ambulance where I answer a series of health-related questions, my anger morphs into sadness. I've been lied to twice. The thought makes my stomach flip-flop, and I can't help but think of all the times I fibbed or played dumb. Surely, I don't make people feel stupid or neglected when they discover the truth, right? My lies are playful. They don't hurt anybody.

At least, I don't think they do . . . .

"Thanks for hanging tight, kiddo." The EMT offers me a high-five that I have no desire to return. "Go home and get some rest."

"Home." I scrunch my face as though I tasted something sour.

What's a home when you can't trust the people who live there?

FIFTEEN
Maggie

"Are you sure you want to go to school?" Mom asks for the millionth time.

She places a plate of eggs, bacon, and watermelon slices in front of me on the table before setting down a massive snot-green smoothie. What is with her asparagus-peanut butter obsession? At least coffee made sense. She cannot honestly tell me she enjoys this vile drink.

Then again, honesty isn't Mom's forte in the Cursed World.

We still have yet to discuss the lying incident from yesterday morning. I guess we're all pretending it never happened. We're also pretending that Mom cares about me, so that's fine.

"You can spend the day with me and Brady." Mom sits across from me.

I avoid eye contact and bite a strip of bacon in half, chewing slowly to savor the flavor. Other than the cinnamon roll with Yolanda, I haven't eaten much since entering the Cursed World. I spent most of yesterday sleeping and hiding out from Mom in the bathroom. I'm starving!

It's hard to believe today is Thursday. Tomorrow is the Fall Equinox Dance.

"I want to see my friends," I say after swallowing.

I need to talk to Sayer about the curse. Something tells me that the last couple of days are just the beginning. Rifling through all the lies I've told, I know I don't want to live any more of them out. I admit, some of them are not my proudest tall tales . . . like when I pretended Grandma Carrie was sick in the hospital to get out of a test last semester. I'd feel awful if that one came true.

The past couple of days has proved that my lies are dangerous.

But a lot of good things came from them, too. Now, I'm BFFs with Laurell, have popularity, straight-A's, Yolanda, and my designer dress from the David Silk Collection.

I struggle with deciding what to do next.

"Fine. Don't skip school," Mom huffs and leaves the table.

I relax when she disappears into her room.

After breakfast, I find another outfit on the floor of my room. I try not to think about what still lurks in my closet. Mom and I head out without Brady, taking his sports car to Magnolia Middle School.

The sun shines bright in the blue, cloudless sky. All evidence of yesterday's blizzard melted away when temperatures reached the low sixties. Only clips of kids playing in the snow on local news stations prove that yesterday existed. Well, and the reports of Elijah Nole surviving a tragic, once-in-a-century-encounter with an iceberg. Thankfully, my name was left off the script.

Driving through Neiwood, my phone buzzes for the thousandth time. I groan, already knowing who is blowing up my text app. Laurell. She thinks bugging me every thirty seconds will spur me into responding, but it does the opposite.

I feel irrationally stubborn about ignoring her and her questions about the yacht. I guess she wanted to be a part of last night's excitement.

What an attention seeker, I think before smiling. We're more alike than I'd like to believe.

A familiar side-braid and environmental t-shirt catches my attention. I do a double take at the person walking out of the small convenience store with two reusable bags. It's the person I've been desperately trying to find since entering the Cursed World.

"Stop the car!" I shout, unbuckling my seatbelt and reaching for the door handle.

"Candice!" Mom stomps on the breaks, causing a car horn to blast behind us.

I hop out of the car before she can drive off, running toward Maggie. I scream her name, heart hammering in my chest. I found her! I finally found Maggie! I've never been more relieved in my life. Now, we can put our heads together and solve this curse!

Maggie slows to a stop and turns around. I barely manage not to crash into her. For the first time since waking up in the Cursed World, I'm face to face with my best friend.

Except she's different now. While she still wears her classic side braid and usual environmental justice shirt, she carries herself in a hunched, mousy sort of way. A plain denim satchel hangs from her shoulder instead of the cute octopus bag that I gave her for her tenth birthday. Her charm bracelet is missing, too, just like mine.

More alarming is the look of pure terror on her face.

"You!" She takes a step back.

What is going on?

"You don't know how glad I am to see you!" I say, pushing past my confusion. "Where have you been? Why haven't you texted me all this time? Why aren't you at school?"

The questions fire from my mouth in a jumbled mess. I wonder if she even understood my words.

She barks out a disbelieving laugh. "You would know. You're the reason!"

"What?" I gape.

I'm the reason she's not at school?

Blood drains from Maggie's cheeks suddenly. She looks over both of my shoulders before spinning around and searching the sidewalk for who knows what. Her hands tremble, shaking the grocery bag.

"Is she here?" Maggie whispers.

"Who?"

"Laurell," she says in a terrified whisper.

"No, just my mom." I point to Brady's idling sports car with Mom behind the wheel.

Maggie's breaths come out in panicked gasps.

"I have to go," she says.

Maggie tries to walk past me, but I step in her way. "Why? What did Laurell do?"

"You mean what both of you did?" she glares.

"Tell me!" I urge, butterflies fluttering in my stomach.

She shakes her head and hisses, "Let me pass!"

"At least give me your phone number."

"Candice Lynn Sky!" I hear my mom shrill. The car idles in a No Parking zone a few cars behind us. "You get over here right now!

Jumping out of a moving vehicle—are you insane?"

Mom's tone is abnormally harsh. In fact, she sounds ready to dropkick me.

Maggie uses the distraction to zip away. I call after her, but she breaks into a run and turns down a corner and out of sight. I reach out as though I could snatch her back, but Mom shouts for me again. I know standing here gobsmacked won't give me answers.

What did Laurell and I do to Maggie in the Cursed World?

***

Later, I slam my belongings on my desk, kick out the chair, and sit down noisily just as the period bell rings. I glare at Mrs. Garcia as she shuts the classroom door, turning toward our English class. I wish she were Mrs. Gulligan so I could give her a piece of my mind!

"Trouble in paradise?" Sayer's voice rouses me.

"How can you tell?" I mutter.

"Well, your iceberg adventure is on every news channel," he says.

I move my arms over my head, a pathetic attempt to shut out the world.

The teacher tells us to pull out our copies of *Bridge to Terabithia,* which I don't have in my bag. I look around for someone who might have an extra copy. Who am I kidding? No middle schooler will have two of the same required reading books.

I lean toward Sayer. "Let's share. I forgot my book."

"No way!" He holds his book as far away from me as possible.

"Oh, come on!" I smack his arm lightly. "It'll be easier for us to talk this way."

"I suppose," Sayer groans dramatically before grinning. His sense of humor doesn't make any sense. Hopefully, he realizes that before he tries stand-up comedy.

I scoot my desk closer, just as Mrs. Garcia announces popcorn reading. I loathe popcorn reading. Students are forced to read passages aloud until the teacher hollers "popcorn" and chooses someone else to torture. Unless you are a newscaster, you spew monotonous blubber that's riddled with stuttering and mispronunciation.

Thankfully, I have Sayer to distract me.

"Do you know a girl named Maggie Fiser? I've been trying to find her, but it's like she dropped off the face of the planet," I whisper, staring at his open book.

Sayer's body becomes abnormally rigid. He stares at me with a horrified expression.

"Haven't you guys done enough?" he whispers.

"What do you mean?" I remember Yolanda's disdain toward Laurell, and I feel dread form in my belly.

Did I do something to hurt my best friend?

"You and your friends are the ones who created that social media page bullying Maggie Fiser. I saw it yesterday."

"What!" I screech, jerking so far back that I fall out of my seat.

Sayer leans his body away as I tumble loudly to the floor. All heads swerve toward us, and he drops his head into his book. Sayer pretends not to know what happened.

That troll.

I'm bullying Maggie? Impossible! I would never do such a thing. In fact, I would die before I let anyone hurt her. She's my best friend! How could a curse do this?

Mrs. Garcia forces a cough, tapping her foot on the carpet impatiently. Hands on her hips, her lips pinch together and resemble a narrow beak.

"Do you need Velcro to sit in your chair properly?" Mrs. Garcia asks without a lick of humor. "Where's your book?"

I stand nervously and wipe the sweat from my palms on my thighs.

"I-I forgot my book at home," I explain. "Sayer was sharing with me, and I guess I lost my balance."

Sayer ducks his head even more, embarrassed to be caught in this mess. His cheeks are pink.

"I'm sure losing your balance was all that happened," she says, gesturing to Sayer's book. "How about you read next, yeah?"

"Sure," I mumble.

I sit, take the book, and start reading. Mrs. Garcia doesn't stop me after just one or two paragraphs. Oh, no. She makes me read aloud an entire page. I mix and skip words, backtrack, and pause randomly until the teacher finally pities me and moves on to the next person. I hear snickers, and even Sayer fails to hold in his laughter. I glare at him before kicking his leg under his desk.

I guess it doesn't matter if the entire world bends to your lies. If you don't change yourself, you will land back in the same situation over and over again. Candy of the Cursed World may be a straight-A student who could've handled reading aloud like it was nothing, but I'm the complete opposite.

I wait a few minutes while other students read aloud, before addressing the bombshell Sayer dropped about Maggie.

"I would never do such a thing," I say under my breath.

Sayer frowns, lips clamped tight. He doesn't believe me.

"Maggie is my best friend. Her pain is my pain." I think back to Maggie's fear-ridden face, and my heart aches. "Tell me more about the social media page," I say after a while.

"You really have no idea?" He sounds almost in awe.

"Apparently not," I lift my chin.

Sayer rubs a hand down his face, sighing. "The page already got taken down, but you can still find screenshots of #TunaBreathMaggie on your best buddy's social media account."

He means Laurell.

My fingers inch toward my phone. Before I know it, I'm on Laurell's social media feed. I search #TunaBreathMaggie in the search engine. The results leave me nauseated.

There are several screenshots of a social media page dedicated to following Maggie discreetly around Magnolia Middle School and recording embarrassing moments throughout her day. One photograph is a blurry closeup of her eating a sandwich. The angle and way she opens her mouth results in two double chins and half-lidded eyes. Someone added fish and barf emojis all around the unsightly photo. Another screenshot shows Maggie opening her gym locker as a tower of canned tuna falls on top of her.

My stomach feels heavy all of a sudden, like someone unloaded a wheelbarrow of bricks in my gut. The pieces fall into place. The reason why Maggie no longer attends our school, her anger toward me, and her fear toward Laurell make sense now.

Maggie was bullied. She had probably gotten herself on Laurell's gossip radar and was targeted with rumors and people going out of their way to be mean to her. Laurell created a social media page dedicated to #TunaBreathMaggie.

Just like the hot sauce incident with Beth Abbot.

"This is because of Mrs. Gulligan!" I exclaim.

Sayer jerks. "You still haven't told me about your curse."

A sharp hush shuts us both up. The teacher sends us both a death glare. I slide my phone into the sleeve of my hoodie as Mrs. Garcia moves toward us. By her stiff posture and reddening face, we are on her last nerve.

I try focusing on the scene in the book, but all I can think about are the screenshots of that horrible website and all those photos of Maggie. Poor, sweet, too-good-and-smart-for-this-world Maggie was bullied.

By none other than Laurell. And *me.*

Laurell hasn't been too terrible since I arrived in the Cursed World, but who knows what she's doing when my back is turned. This must be what Yolanda didn't want to talk about at the cafe yesterday—why she didn't like the idea of me hanging out with Laurell. Yolanda must know about us bullying Maggie.

My stomach churns. I swallow to stop from throwing up.

Oh, I wish I could take back every moment my lies put Maggie in an awkward position. I wish I could take back putting Elijah Nole ahead of our friendship. Most importantly, I wish I had appreciated how one-of-a-kind and amazing Maggie is.

I clench my fists, lips parting in a snarl. How dare Laurell! How dare she hurt my best friend! She's lucky I don't give her a #KnuckleSandwich!

"Dude, you look like you're gonna Hulk-out on somebody," Sayer whispers.

I take a few breaths, forcing myself to relax. Pink crescent indents form where my fingernails dig painfully into my skin. No one hurts my best friend and gets away with it!

Laurell isn't fully to blame, though. My lies made the Cursed World the way it is, and apparently for each lie to come true, certain aspects of my life shifted to fit the mold. To right the wrongs I have created, I have no other choice than to follow what Sayer suggested in the recreation center's infirmary.

"I need to break Mrs. Gulligan's curse." I lock gazes with Sayer. "Will you help me?"

He straightens in his seat, lips tugging up in a lopsided smile. “Meet me at the abandoned lighthouse after school.”

SIXTEEN

Reversing the Curse

The tide is still low enough to expose the long mound of boulders to the lighthouse. In an hour or so, the tide will submerge the natural bridge underwater, and we'll either have to wait until tomorrow or swim back. The latter option is *not* happening. Sayer better have a good plan.

Mollusks and anemones flourish in the pools between the jagged, barnacle encrusted rocks. Spiral sea snails crawl in between them. The sour smell of rotting crab mixes with briny seaweed. At one point, we stumble past a starfish, and I have the urge to crouch down and poke around some of the deeper crevices.

One time on this ridge, Maggie and I found a young ruby octopus camouflaging itself in a discarded water bottle. It was the first time we had seen one in the wild, and it had quickly become Maggie's favorite animal. My chest swells from the memory. I can't wait to break this curse. I miss her.

I jump from one rock to another, crossing over a tidepool, and my foot slips and lands into the sun-warmed water. I click my tongue, annoyed, and lift my soaking sneakers—the ones I bought with Yolanda—to shake the droplets off.

Sayer reaches the lighthouse's island with ease, and he grins triumphantly over his shoulder. He laughs as I fall into yet another pool. I'm tempted to grab some seagrass and lob it at his overconfident face. I push down that urge, scrabbling the rocks on all fours until I reach the grassy bank.

I sit on the damp grass and yank my shoes off, dumping out the excess water and wringing my socks. Sayer snaps his fingers at me.

"Hurry up before someone notices us!" he says.

"Okay, okay," I grumble. Socks dangling in hand, I shove my bare feet back into my shoes and stomp after him.

The lighthouse is a white one-story house connected to a standard white brick tower with a red stripe painted around its middle. At the top, a steel railing surrounds an old lamp beacon. Sayer leads us past the house to a side door that leads into the tower.

"We're going inside the abandoned lighthouse?" I peer through a window, noting a lack of dust and cobwebs. That's odd. The building hasn't been in use for over fifty years.

"The lighthouse isn't actually abandoned." Sayer pulls out a set of keys. "It's retired."

"Uh . . ." I watch with surprise as he unlocks the door and pushes it open. "How do you have keys for the lock?" I ask.

"My mom works for the State Park, and she helps maintain the lighthouse," he explains. "They're waiting on a grant to restore the lighthouse so it can be open for the public."

The smell of copper penetrates my nose as I step inside. A rusted staircase spirals up the circular room. Our footsteps echo off the chipped-paint walls, decorated with raunchy graffiti and limestone. The room is remarkably clean, despite the efforts of rowdy teenagers, and I spot a mop, bucket, and cart of cleaning supplies in an open closet next to the stairs.

"So your mom takes care of the lighthouse." The cool air pricks at my skin, and I cross my arms over my chest. "That still doesn't explain why you have keys."

"I swiped a copy when I was researching my curse," he says. "I didn't want anyone thinking I was crazy for reading about witches and magic."

"Gotcha," I nod.

Sayer gestures toward the stairs. The bolts whine as he ascends, and I gulp as I clutch the vibrating rails. The open-air gaps between the steps make me nervous, so I'm careful not to accidentally overstep and slip a foot through them.

We pass through a room similar to the first floor, barren except for an empty bookshelf and a vintage sofa covered in a plastic sheet. A rolled-up rug is propped upright in the closet, and Sayer informs me that we're in the living room. When ships still used the beacon above us, the lighthouse keeper stayed six weeks at a time, depending on the weather, followed by a two-week break. Apparently, the house connecting to the tower has a kitchen and bathroom.

We reach a door at the top of the staircase, Sayer fiddling with his keys. I look over the railing. If the flimsy staircase decides to break, Sayer and I will most definitely fall to our deaths. A wave of dizziness hits me, and I yank my head back, taking long, deep breaths.

"Are you coming?" Sayer's voice startles me out of my pre-panic attack.

He ventures into the room, leaving me alone on the stairs. I scramble up the final steps, leap onto the stone floor, and slam the door shut. The force of the sound causes thunder to clap down the tower.

"Yikes, Candy!" Sayer exclaims.

"Sorry," I pant, looking around the room.

A wooden bed frame with no mattress sits between a matching dresser and a chairless desk. An old-fashioned oil lamp dangles from a hook, and the walls are untouched by teenage rebellion. A wooden ladder in the corner connects the bedroom to the upstairs gallery.

The air is thicker up here, full of dust particles that shimmer in the light descending outside the windows. Unlike the rooms below, four glass panels provide directional views of the lighthouse's surroundings. I can see everything from up here. Morgan Bay and Neiwood. The California coastline. The Pacific Ocean.

"Beautiful," I whisper, peering out of the window overlooking the ocean's endless glittering water.

Maggie would love this.

"The gallery is better." Sayer jabs a thumb toward the ladder.

"Oh, I bet! Can we go up there?" I ask.

The ladder steps are partially eroded from someone climbing up and down it for decades. It's still safer than the stairs, so I'm willing to take the risk for an amazing view.

"Someone will notice us," Sayers says, and I frown with disappointment.

His backpack slides off his shoulders and thumps heavily to the ground. He takes out his phone and extends it high above his head, checking for a signal. He mutters "no bars" and returns it to his pocket. I test my luck but have the same results.

Sayer retrieves a spiral notebook and opens it to a fresh page. He sits on the ground, and I join him. With a pen, he writes "Candy's Curse" on the header. I already know where this is going.

"We should discuss all the changes caused by your curse," Sayer says. "That way, we're both on the same page and can pick out similar cases from the books."

"Way ahead of you." I reveal the list I've been updating frequently throughout my time in the Cursed World.

Sayer reads each bullet. His eyes widen. I wonder what's more shocking to him, the elves or that a yacht hit an iceberg in California.

"Your situation is much more extreme than mine was," he says after a while. "It's as though your entire life was rewritten. Nothing major changed for me. Well, except for the money."

"And your face?" I add.

He glares, pointing to his perfectly smooth cheeks. Not a zit in sight. "Puberty, thank you very much. Something every adolescent goes through," he snarks.

I fight back a laugh. Poor Sayer. We've certainly reached the age of pizza faces and onion armpits.

"What happened with your curse?" I ask.

"I just told you."

I roll my eyes. "Yeah, you confirmed the rumor about money turning into leaves when you touch it, but what about the little details? How long did you have your curse? What consequences did you face? Were there any lasting effects? Does anyone else know about what happened to you? Or is everyone clueless, like with my curse?"

"One question at a time!" Sayer says. Slowly, he takes off his gloves, flexing his fingers. "First thing's first, you need to understand why I'm helping you. Do you have a dollar?"

Anticipation builds as I reach for the wallet in my purse. I don't have a dollar, but I do have a handful of change, so I scoop the coins up and pass them to Sayer. Holding my breath, I watch the coins curl inward and morph from shiny silver metal into acorn caps.

Once again, I smell black licorice.

Sayer tips his hand, letting them clatter to the ground. Our eyes lock, and I realize a painful truth about the boy standing in front of me. It's a truth that causes me to feel both fear and panic.

Sayer never broke his curse.

The acorn caps taunt me from the middle of the floor. In my mind, their wide mouths animate and laugh wickedly at my latest crisis. If Sayer never broke his curse, does that mean I might be stuck in the Cursed World forever?

"No, no, no!" My heart ignites with terror.

I kick my feet out and propel myself backward until I hit the wall behind me. Curling my knees to my chest, I thread my fingers through my hair and pull. A mumbled "no" rides each exhale as I hyperventilate.

This can't be happening! I can't be stuck in the Cursed World forever! I've been here for four days, and I've already encountered three near-death experiences. And yes, I'm counting my battle with the elves.

A touch on my head startles me, and I look up at Sayer's concerned face. Standing over me, his hand rests on my hair.

"Tell me everything," I demand.

"Right." He licks his lips, dropping his gaze. "I know what I did was wrong, so save whatever lecture you might have. Also, my reasoning is irrelevant. You don't need to know why, except that what I did wasn't for me."

"You're stalling." I break away from him, crossing my legs as I lean against the wall. "C'mon, tell me already."

Sayer blows out a long breath. With a grimace, he whispers, "I stole money . . . from Mrs. Gulligan."

"You did what!" My eyes widen into saucers. "How much money are we talking about?"

"An entire paycheck." He scratches the back of his head, looking down at his shoes. "I swiped it from her purse when she was out of the classroom."

"No freaking way." I cover my mouth with my hand, shocked. "Why on Earth would you do such a thing?"

"I told you my reasoning doesn't matter. Stealing is stealing."

"I get that," I say. "But you can't drop a bombshell like that on me and not explain why."

Sayer is quiet for a moment. He rubs a hand over his curls, clearly debating if he wants to tell me. Eventually, his body sags. He picks up an acorn cap, hurling it across the room.

"Last year, my dad got into a car accident that crushed his leg. He was out of work for almost six months, and I overheard my parents talking about falling behind on the mortgage with just one income. I guess the insurance was taking forever to kick in or something—I really don't know anything about insurance.

"Anyway, they were thinking about moving to Montana, because it's a cheaper place to live and closer to my grandparents. I didn't want to move. All my friends are in California. When I saw Mrs. Gulligan's check poking out of her purse, I thought I could help my parents."

"That's . . . wow," I whistle, not knowing what else to say.

"It's no excuse for stealing." Sayer's cheeks darken as he flushes. "The ironic thing is I couldn't cash the check without Mrs. Gulligan's ID and signature. I tried lying that she was my grandma, but the bank teller still refused. When I realized my mistake, I planned on returning the check, but I lost it."

"No!" I cry.

Sayer nods. "Mrs. Gulligan found out I stole her check and cursed me. I've been unable to touch any sort of money for over a year. I guess

I should be grateful that she didn't call the police on me.

"I feel so bad about it. I've been saving money to pay her back. I spent all summer mowing lawns, running bake sales, and washing cars. Just last weekend, I finally earned enough. I planned to give the money back to Mrs. Gulligan on Monday, but then she disappeared." He walks to the window next to me and leans on the sill, staring down blankly at Morgan Bay.

Sayer's story is out of this world. Stealing from a teacher takes a lot of guts, and not in a good way. Sure, his intentions were pure, but he's right—stealing is stealing.

Too bad he lost that check.

"Your turn." He spins around and raises a brow.

I hum, debating where to start and how much I want to tell. We'd be here all day if I went through every single lie I've ever told. I better stick to the lies from the list.

"Mrs. Gulligan cursed me so that all of my lies would come true," I say. Then, I detail everything that's happened to me in the Cursed World and how it correlates to fibs I've told in the past.

When I finish, Sayer's mouth falls open.

I rub my wrist self-consciously, aware that my friendship bracelet is missing. "Y-yeah. It's a lot."

"People seriously believed your lies?" He sounds amazed.

"More or less . . . mostly yes."

"And the elves?" He points to my list. "You're not pranking me?"

"Of course not!" I scoff. "That's not something I would lie about."

He pinches his lips together and gives me a look. I realize my mistake. If I had taken responsibility for cleaning my room, the elves wouldn't exist in the Cursed World to begin with.

"Not in this situation," I add, nervously swirling my finger in the dust on the ground, doodling little circles.

"We should talk to the elves." Sayer says, returning my list.

I grip the paper in shock, crumpling it. "You're kidding, right?"

"They were sent—conjured, whatever—by Mrs. Gulligan. They might know something about breaking your curse. Plus, they could give the money I saved to Mrs. Gulligan."

"They're animals! Vicious, rabid beasts!"

"Do you want to be stuck in the Cursed World forever?" Sayer crosses his arms.

Every cell in my body screams that this is a bad idea. We're not elf whisperers! The moment I let them loose, they're going to go back to destruction and mayhem.

But we have no other clues, and I don't want to risk another lie coming true. Mrs. Gulligan's curse might kill me!

I sigh and rub my eyes tiredly. Finally, I nod with agreement for the plan. There's no doubt in my mind that I'm going to regret this.

"We better hurry before the tide comes in any further and we have to swim to shore," Sayer says.

I shiver from the thought of swimming. "Right. Let's go!"

SEVENTEEN
Truce

Mom always told me to think before I do something stupid, weigh the rewards and consequences, and then make a decision. She usually says this after I'm caught in a lie. It's a recycled lecture followed by a recycled list of chores. I've never considered following the advice. I ignored it when I stole her credit card for a bikini. I ignored it when I started hiding my grades. And I certainly ignored it when I lied to Mrs. Gulligan.

However, as Sayer and I arrive in the destroyed birthday cake bedroom, my brain races with all the consequences of what will happen when I open the closet door. I layer myself with extra clothes for protection and grab the paddle from under the bed, slowly creeping toward the dresser blocking the elves from invasion.

"Is this really necessary?" Sayer helps me move the dresser out of the way.

"We should be wearing bulletproof armor," I say. "Trust me, the elves are awful."

I lift my hand to the doorknob, but the tension in my body stops me short. Come on, Candy, you can do this! They're six-inch little matchsticks and you're a Godzilla compared to them. Blast them away with your paddle again if they get too rowdy. You've got this! Just move your hand forward. Slowly, slowly, slowly—

"Oh, for the love of . . ." Sayer pushes past me, my arm still outstretched. "Let me do it!"

I scrunch my eyes shut and recoil from the glide of the door against the carpet as it opens. I expect the elves to rush out with their yellow eyes, mangy beards, and horrible attempts at makeshift weapons. All that hits me, though, is a foul stench of cat pee and feces. I haven't seen Pickles since entering the Cursed World, so he couldn't have been accidentally locked up.

Did the elves use the closet as a bathroom? Disgusting!

"There's no one in here," Sayer says, hand covering his nose.

My eyes snap open. I inch toward the closet and take in the metal racks. The hangers are empty, and shoes and accessories are strewn across the floor.

No elves in sight.

"Impossible! I know they're here. I heard them making strange noises all night. Hopefully, they didn't get loose."

Of course, the apartment would be trashed if they had. Maybe they dug a hole into the next apartment? Good riddance! Even if Sayer thinks they might have a clue to our curses, I'm glad we have to find another way.

I turn to leave the closet when I hear Brutus Hurst. "Attack!"

From the ceiling, eight tiny bodies drop and land on my head and shoulders. I scream as the elves grip my hair and yank strands of it like horse reins. They shout incoherent words and pound their fists against my face and neck.

I stumble out of the closet, swatting them unsuccessfully. Their hold is too strong. My foot catches on a pile of clothes and paper, and I lose balance. Barely raising my hands in front of me, I break my fall against the ground.

The elves finally let go, and I hear them scamper away. I push myself up, thinking I finally escaped them. However, the elves disappear back into the closet before emerging with unfolded hangers and clothes tied together into makeshift rope.

Brutus Hurst barrels toward me, his butter knife raised high above his head. He emits an animalistic battle cry. I scramble backwards when I realize they plan on stabbing me with the coat hangers. The nightstand stops me.

"Help!" I shout to Sayer who is standing by the closet in disbelief. Next to him, I spot the paddle I dropped earlier. "For the love of everything—stop them!"

Sayer blinks out of his stupor. He leaps forward and attempts to cut the elves off, but they slip around his ankles. I cover my face as Brutus Hurst leaps onto my leg.

Thwack!

The dull blade of the elf's knife bounces off my knee. The attack itself was painless.

However, the sharp jabs of the unfolded hangers are like needles pricking my skin. I twist my body until I'm curled on the floors, arms protecting my head.

"Get them off!" I shriek, scrunching my eyes shut.

I hear a grunt, and the faint weight on my hip disappears. Another "oof" results in less stabbing hangers. I risk a squint and see Sayer standing above me.

He kicks and slaps the elves off of me. He snatches Brutus Hurst's butter knife, lifting the elf when the stubborn thing won't let go, and tosses him onto the bed. The other elves clamber back onto me, but they don't last long before a second date with Sayer's foot. The entire time, Sayer collects their weapons.

The elves' efforts slow after their third wave of attacks, and soon we come to a standstill. Panting and weaponless, the elves bare their jagged teeth despite their slumped and defeated shoulders. Brutus Hurst slides down the bed, turning toward us with eyes watering with anger.

"You are even more rotten than Mrs. Gulligan told us!" Spittle sprays with the force of his words. "We've been without food and water for days!"

"I was attacked by a bunch of garden gnomes claiming to be elves! What was I supposed to do?" I push myself up, stomping to my feet.

Brutus Hurst growls and lifts his hand to cue his comrades for another round of attacks. Sayer senses their intentions and holds his hands up in mock surrender. He shifts in front of me so that I'm out of view.

"Can we call a truce?" he suggests.

Brutus snorts before spitting out a glob of green phlegm. "We are far past any truce."

"You're hungry right? What if Candy makes something to eat? As an apology?" Sayer reasons.

"I'm not apolo—" I start to say, but Sayer swings his foot back and kicks my shin with his heel. Ouch!

"You think you can bribe us with some mediocre meal? Ha!" the elf snarls. "We require a feast! Enough food and drink to feed a hundred human men! Only then will we consider the thought of a truce."

"I'm sure we can figure out something," Sayer says, turning toward me. "What do you have to eat?"

Before I can respond, Brutus Hurst cuts in. "You are not understanding our request. The feast we want is not something two bratty kids can put together. It must be grand enough for a king!"

Sayer frowns and looks to me for help.

"Why don't we order take out," I suggest. "We can use my credit card."

If it bought me a designer dress for over $1,700, then it should cover the kind of feast the elves desire. Plus, I can't imagine the elves will eat that much food. They're six inches tall, for crying out loud!

"That works. I'll look up restaurants that offer delivery." Sayer unlocks his phone and begins swiping. "Do you know how to use a phone?" he asks Brutus Hurst.

"We're elves, not gnomes living under rocks. Of course we know how to use a phone!" the elf snaps.

Sayer passes his phone to him. "Order whatever you like."

A murmur of excitement fills the room, and all the elves crowd Brutus Hurst, blurting their food requests. Their words jumble together, demanding pizza, flapjacks, and enchiladas. Sayer and I wait for what feels like an eternity, silently entranced by the strange creatures, before Brutus Hurst passes the phone back.

"Hopefully you have enough to pay," he singsongs, lips curling into a sharp-toothed smile.

***

I'm dreaming. That's the only explanation for why fifteen food delivery workers stand in the hallway, carrying towers of take-out boxes. Maybe that's what the Cursed World is—all a dream.

The hallway is loud with chatter, the workers just as shocked at the amount of food as I am. A few of Brady's neighbors poke their heads out of their apartments to watch the commotion. I wave awkwardly at them before I hand the first delivery guy my credit card.

"Is there a wedding or something?" he asks, inserting my card into a card reader.

A wedding certainly sounds more believable than hosting a feast for eight savage elves. I open my mouth to fake-confirm his suspicion, but a series of violent coughs stop me. I turn away, covering my mouth with my elbow until the accompanying black licorice smell subsides.

"This is seriously getting annoying." I wipe spit from my lips.

The card reader chirps, and I expect a receipt to spit out, but the guy frowns and tries my card again. I wring my hands, waiting to know the payment has been approved. He hands it back. His face is full of dread.

"It's been declined," he says. "Insufficient funds."

"That's impossible! There was enough money the other day," I say.

"Well, it's gone now."

The hallway becomes eerily quiet as all the food delivery workers watch our interaction. I feel the hair on my neck rise. I try handing the credit card back, wanting him to run it again, but he shakes his head. He refuses to take it.

"Do you have another way to pay?" he asks.

I hear someone behind the guy mutter, "She better or my manager is gonna call the cops."

"Wait here," I say quickly and retreat back into the apartment.

Mom and Brady must have money somewhere. I can't believe my card has been declined. I used it the other day to buy the dress! Maybe the dress was too much money and I spent all the funds? Or maybe Brady cut me off when he realized how much I spent? I never really got his approval.

I go into their room for the first time since entering the Cursed World. It's L-shaped, with a granite, double-bathroom sink, bathroom, and jacuzzi attached. I'm shocked by the amount of dirty clothes strewn across the floor, as well as the makeup mom left open on the counter. My mom would never let her room get this way. Her clothes are vacuum sealed in plastic bags, and her makeup is never in sight, always stowed in a lidded container.

Pinching my nose, I use a hanger to remove dirty boxers from the nightstand before opening the drawer. Unfortunately, all I find are receipts for various clubs and bars next to a camouflage lighter. Mom's side is no better. It's stuffed with magazines and spilled neon nail polish.

I check a few other places in the room before I hear pounding knocks from the apartment front door. I don't have a lot of time. The delivery workers are growing impatient.

Sayer emerges from the birthday cake room.

"What's going on?" he asks, making sure none of the elves follow him out.

"My card has been declined," I say.

He gasps, "You can't be serious."

"There's about fifteen delivery guys in the hallway about to call the police if we don't pay them soon."

Sayer thinks for a moment before he disappears back into the bedroom. He returns with his backpack and digs around inside. He pulls out an envelope, before he hands it to me.

"Use this," he says.

Inside the envelope is more cash than I've ever seen in my life.

"Is this the money you saved?" I gawk.

"Yes, two thousand and five hundred dollars, exactly," he sighs.

"What about giving it back to Mrs. Gulligan?"

"I've lived this long with the curse. What's another couple of months?" he tries to smile, but a crack in his voice tells me he's trying to hold himself together.

I place a hand on his shoulder. "I'll help you. I promise."

I return to the impatient delivery persons with the envelope of cash. Slowly, I pass out what we owe. The food is carried inside and packed onto the kitchen table and counters. Soon, there's not enough room, and the living room becomes an ocean of pizza boxes, burritos, Thai food, and platters of seafood from the most expensive Cajun restaurant in town.

The money in the envelope dwindles, and by the time the final food delivery worker is paid, only a quarter and a few pennies are left. I stare at the coins with disbelief. The elves really ordered two thousand and five hundred dollars worth of food. They are six inches tall, for crying out loud! Do they really expect to eat all this? Or is this a punishment for locking them in the closet?

Sayer picks through the boxes in the kitchen, and I approach him grimly. I hold out the change.

He stares at it for a moment, shoving his hands in his pocket before turning away. I hear Sayer sniff, his shoulders shuddering, and I feel the urge to hug him. All that work—a year's worth of saving money—all gone.

We shouldn't have let the elves have free rein to order food.

"Let's get this feast going," Sayer mutters.

Not knowing what to say, I help him gather armfuls of food, carrying them into the birthday cake room. It takes us thirty minutes to pack everything inside. The elves dive into the food right away, and by the time we're done, there's only a small circle of space for us to sit.

Sayer leans against the wall next to me, our shoulders pressed together, and we rest paper plates with uneaten greasy pizza on our laps. He seems dazed by the eight smacking mouths that demolish four whole pies in less than twenty minutes. The elves are quite pleased with the feast.

Sayer sets his plate aside and scooches closer to the elves. Brutus Hurst narrows his eyes, but he doesn't draw a weapon like he and his companions did each time I barged into the room with stacks of food.

Locking the elves in my closet without food, water, and a proper toilet rubbed them the wrong way.

I do not look forward to cleaning up their mess.

Sayer crosses his legs and nervously rubs his gloved fingers on his knees.

"Brutus Hurst, sir, do you know anything about Mrs. Gulligan's curse?" he asks.

The elf uses his pinky nail to dig spinach from his teeth. "Maybe, maybe not," he says.

That's helpful.

Not.

"What about breaking our curses?" Sayer presses on.

The elf hums. He points to me and asks for a quarter. I toss him the one left over from Sayer's savings.

"Flip a coin. Heads, I tell you. Tails, I don't," Brutus Hurst says.

Sayer frowns. "You'll have to flip it. If I touch the coin, it will turn into an acorn cap."

"Are you sure about that?"

Sayer reaches out with trembling fingers. His hand hovers over the quarter, eyes flickering to Brutus Hurst to see if this is some sort of trick, before he grasps the coin. I lean forward, waiting for the silver to curl and turn brown. Nothing happens.

"I don't understand," Sayer whispers.

"You, Sayer Lafayette, have broken your curse."

"B-But how?"

Brutus Hurst flicks a half-eaten pepperoni slice off his chest before he answers. "To break your curse, you need to learn what it's like to lose money you've shed blood, sweat, and tears for, just like what happened to Mrs. Gulligan when you stole her paycheck."

"I wanted to return that money to her, though. If I spent it on the feast, doesn't that still mean she's out two thousand and five hundred dollars?"

"She got the school to write her a new check."

"Oh." Sayer positions the quarter on his thumb and flicks it into the air. It somersaults several times before he catches it, slapping it onto the top of his hand. When he pulls away, the coin shows heads.

Yes!

"Bummer." Brutus Hurst takes a bite of his pizza. "I was kind of hoping you'd have to suffer a little longer before I'd have to tell you," he says to me. "At least Sayer did what he did to help someone he loved. You, on the other hand, not only lied to get what you wanted, but also took pleasure in fooling people."

"Yeah, I get it." I feel heat rise to my cheeks, and I roll a dropped olive across the floor.

"Do you, though?" The elf raises a brow. "Do you understand the damage lying causes?"

For a moment, I think he's talking about all the bad things that happened to me in the Cursed World, but then I remember how hurt I was when Elijah and Mom lied to me. Then, there was also the fact that Candy of the Cursed World lied to cover Laurell when she was caught bullying Maggie. *That* crushes me more than any rejection from Elijah Nole or negligence from Mom ever could.

"I do now," I whisper.

Brutus Hurst tosses his dirty plate aside and brings the straw of his root beer to his lips. He takes several loud gulps and belches. I rub my bracelet-less wrist, wishing he'd hurry up.

"To break your curse," Brutus Hurst says finally, his voice lowering, "you must confess."

"To my lies?" I say. "That seems easy enough."

"Is it though?" Brutus Hurst asks. "Confessing means accepting the consequences that you have selfishly avoided for almost your entire life."

I shift uncomfortably.

The elf continues, "Plus, you cannot confess to just anyone. You have to confess to the people you lied to."

"That's impossible!" I screech. I've lied to pretty much everyone I know! Some people were just bypassers in my life—a clerk at a grocery store or a nurse at the doctors' office. Who knows if I'll ever meet those strangers again?

"Then I guess you'll be cursed forever," Brutus Hurst says. "Mrs. Gulligan wasn't specific when she revealed how to break your curse, but knowing how she works, you will have to make your confession big."

"Make it big," I repeat his words, thinking about different ways I could accomplish this.

"A news broadcast?" Sayer suggests. "Except, how will you get on TV?"

"I could ask Yolanda, but her talk show doesn't start for a while," I muse, stroking my chin.

"Plus, she's a product of your lie," Sayer points out. "Using her is kinda the easy way out."

I agree with Sayer's assumption. Based on how he broke his curse, Mrs. Gulligan wouldn't want my solution to come easily. Also, I don't think making it on the news will work. Most of my more outrageous lies are from recently, since my obsession with Elijah Nole began. More specifically, I've lied the most since learning about the Fall Equinox Dance. Based on that timeline, I lied to teachers, peers, and my parents. Except for Mom, hardly anyone I know watches the news.

An idea hits me, and I jump to my feet.

"The dance!" I cry.

Sayer stands up too, kicking aside a few of the elves' empty takeout boxes.

"What about the dance?" he asks.

Stomach full of butterflies, I whisper, "I know exactly how I will confess."

Cursed World

- I live in a super nice apartment with a man named Brady.
- I have a dream room and a dream closet.
- ~~I'm friends best friends with Laurell~~. Laurell is a jerk! A big bully!
- I have a famous cousin named Yolanda Nox.
- I'm a straight-A student.

- ~~ELIJAH NOLE IS MY BOYFRIEND!~~
- ~~ELIJAH NOLE IS MY BOYFRIEND!~~
- ~~ELIJAH NOLE IS MY BOYFRIEND!~~

  ~~This totally deserved three bullet points.~~

- ~~I'M GOING TO THE DANCE WITH ELIJAH NOLE!~~
- I'd rather go to the dance with Brutus Hurst than Elijah Nole!
- Mrs. Gulligan does not exist.
- I'm a frequent shopper at David Silk Collection.
- I have a credit card!
- Elves attacked me. Elves! They exist!
- I'm a champion swimmer . . . not really.
- Maggie is MIA.
- An iceberg in California
- Maggie was bullied by Laurell . . . and I helped.

EIGHTEEN

The Fall Equinox Dance

"There has to be at least one pair of shoes around here!" I say. I've been searching for half an hour. All of the shoes I—or Candy of the Cursed World—own disappeared. I didn't need the smell of Mrs. Gulligan's magic to tell me why.

"Of all the lies that came true, why'd it have to be this." I feel like a broken record. "And right before Laurell is supposed to pick me up, too."

It's 4:20 p.m. The Fall Equinox Dance starts in forty minutes. Of course, nothing in the Cursed World goes my way, so the lie I told Mom about missing all my shoes so I could buy a new pair came true. I can't even find any of Mom's or Brady's!

An elf snickers next to me as he chomps on leftover takeout. Surprisingly, the elves have done a fair number on the food. When Mom and Brady didn't come home last night or this morning—much to my relief—I ditched school and spent the day, dare I say, *cleaning* the apartment. I never thought I'd see the day where I voluntarily cleaned anything, but here I am in a somewhat organized room after piling the communal apartment dumpster high with trash bags.

I stick my tongue out at the elf before standing up and searching one more time for a pair of shoes. No luck. I plop on the sofa and run a hand through my hair, wondering what I should do. I will look ridiculous going to the dance without shoes, but I guess I have no choice.

My phone rings. The caller ID shows that it's Laurell. Anger boils in my stomach at the sight of her name. I'm reminded of what she did to

Maggie, and how I supposedly lied to cover for her. I tried getting out of riding with her to the dance by asking Sayer if we could go together, but he had robotics club and wouldn't get out until later. In our text exchange earlier, he told me he brought his dance outfit to school and would change in the locker room.

I'm on my own.

I take a few breaths and answer the call.

"We're here!" Laurell cheers. "Hurry and get down here! You're not gonna believe the limo Elijah's parents rented."

"I'll be down in a moment," I grate.

I hang up the phone before Laurell can say anything more. Returning to my room, I find a pair of socks and slide them onto my feet. It looks stupid, but it's better than going barefoot.

I glance around the room, noticing Brutus Hurst on my bed, feet propped up with a half-eaten chicken skewer on his chest. He hums a happy tune with his eyes closed. The other elves wreak havoc on the room that I spent all of yesterday cleaning.

Already, papers, books, and trophies litter the floor. I roll my eyes, poking Brutus Hurst's shoulder gently.

He cracks an eye open.

"Stay in the bedroom," I say. "I don't want Mom or Brady finding out about you."

"Whatever you say, Pinocchio," he quips, and my eye twitches at the nickname.

***

Laurell waves through the window of a limousine as I exit Brady's apartment building. My mouth drops at the size of our ride. It's at least thirty feet long! The driver, wearing a black suit and chauffeur hat, opens the back door as I approach.

Inside, purple lights illuminate a long, white leather bench that stretches along one side of the limo. A bar, plasma TV, and built-in gaming computer take up the other side. The synthetic yet pleasant citrus scent causes me to breathe deep, and I wonder if there's an incense diffuser hidden somewhere inside. Pop music blares from the speakers on the roof.

"Cand-ee!" Laurell pounces on me, grabbing my hand and dragging me further into the limo.

She wears a red mermaid gown with lace sleeves and a beaded lattice along the collar. A diamond necklace rests on her exposed neck, and she has teardrop earrings and a bracelet to match. Her blonde hair is curled, stacked on top of her head, and studded with crystals. Laurell tops her look with eyeliner wings and a cherry lipstick.

A few days ago, I would have melted at being so close to the beautiful queen of Magnolia Middle School. Now, it takes all my willpower not to shrug away from her touch.

I only notice a third person with us in the limo when I sit down. His back is hunched, and his face is pinched like a grouchy elf. Elijah Nole. I feel myself bristle when he mumbles a half-hearted hello. He refuses to look at me.

"What is he doing here!" I demand.

"Fulfilling my end of the bargain," he grumbles.

Laurell takes the spot next to me, not bothering with the seatbelt. "Don't worry, I convinced him that you could always tell Yolanda how he dumped you before the dance," she says, turning her attention to Elijah. "Then, you'll never get on her talk show."

"You were in on this?" I ask her.

"Uh, you and I came up with the deal together, remember?" Laurell leans over and grabs two lemon sodas. She cracks them both open and holds one out. "I helped you, so you could help me get on Yolanda's show, too."

I should be surprised, but I'm not. Their greed knows no bounds. The idea of their scheming makes me a little sick to my stomach. However, I remind myself that I'm not much better. That's why the Cursed World exists, after all.

"Candy, where are your shoes?" Laurell gasps.

I look down at my socks. "I have no idea."

"You forgot, didn't you!" she screeches. "How can you just forget your shoes? Please tell me this is a joke and you're hiding a pair in your purse."

"I didn't forget," I say. "All of my shoes disappeared."

"What about the paparazzi?" she asks.

My grip tightens on the can, and soda spills onto my hand. I gasp and quickly slurp up the mess. I forget about holding my purse in my lap, and it falls to the ground. Instead of my usual contents, lobster shells dump out.

Laurell screams and jumps away.

I blink several times at the putrid carcasses. I honestly have no words. This is totally the result of those blasted elves. Oh, when I get home, I'm barricading them back in the closet.

How did I not notice the smell from my purse before?

Gagging breaks my shock, and I look over at Elijah. He clasps a hand over his mouth, body heaving as he threatens to throw up. Seeing him like that gives me pleasure, and I'm tempted to throw the lobster shell at him as revenge for breaking my heart.

"What were you saying about paparazzi?" I ask as though everything is fine and dandy.

This really isn't the worst or strangest thing that's happened to me in the Cursed World.

They ignore my question.

"Why do you have lobster shells in your purse?" Laurell screeches.

"We gotta stop the limo." Elijah hacks. "We gotta throw them away."

"You're not a fan of seafood?" I nudge the lobster shell with my toe and grin when Laurell and Elijah shriek.

"You are disgusting, Candice Lynn Sky!" Laurell exclaims.

I shrug and look out the window. We're only a couple turns away from the school, so there's no point in making the driver pull over now. Plus, I'll admit that I enjoy their discomfort. It's payback for deceiving me and hurting me and my best friend.

My biggest concern right now is the paparazzi. Elijah Nole's fans are vicious hyenas. I know because I used to be one. As soon as a picture of me with Elijah hits the internet, I'll be picked apart. *Why didn't she style her hair? Is she not wearing any makeup? Where are her shoes?*

And then there's my favorite comment: *Elijah Nole could find someone better.*

I don't want anyone thinking I'm dating that jerkasaurus. Thus, I need to avoid the paparazzi at all costs. Otherwise, I'll lose what little confidence I have for my plan at the dance.

As we pull into the school's bus lane, Laurell and Elijah still retching, I spot the security guard blocking a group of reporters with microphones and giant cameras. They raise their cameras whenever a car drops off a student, deflating when it's not Elijah Nole. My stomach churns at the sight of them. Even though the windows are tinted, I slouch in my seat so they can't see me.

The limo turns into the school lot before coming to a stop. Voices filter in from outside, growing loud at our arrival. Laurell and Elijah don't wait for the driver to come around and open their doors. They clamber out and gasp fresh air.

Huh. Turns out the rotting lobster works in my favor. I'm alone now and can make an escape.

I slip through the passenger door facing the road, away from the paparazzi, and sneak around the back of the limo. Sharp pebbles poke the soles of my feet, and I bite my lip to keep from making a sound. Questions fire at Elijah Nole. *How are you feeling after the boating incident? Are you suffering from food poisoning? Where is your date for the dance?* I feel a little guilty for ditching him.

Not.

I peek around to make sure no one is watching, before I launch forward out of the drop-off circle, onto the sidewalk, and through the school's lawn. I cringe when mud squelches under my feet, soaking through my socks and between my toes.

"Cand-ee!" I hear Laurell call, but I'm already halfway to the entrance.

I flash my student ID at the check-in booth and race inside. I jump around bodies and sail through the hallways. A group of girls pose for selfies, and I photobomb them by accident. I hear an irritated "hey!" but I turn a corner before there are any repercussions.

Music grows louder the further I push through the crowds. Balloons arch across the ceiling, and posters for the Fall Equinox Dance plaster the walls. Up ahead, a cork of students block the gymnasium doors, slowly filling inside.

I don't have time to wait for them. Tendrils of nervousness suffocate my thoughts, and I start to doubt my plan. Not only do I have no idea if this is going to work, but the thought of standing in front of everyone and confessing sends my heart racing. Goosebumps form up my arm.

I head for the girls locker room instead. In the side hallway, only a handful of students linger. The locker room is quiet except for the bass of the music booming faintly. Air from the ceiling fan cools my skin. A layer of sweat covers my face from getting so worked up.

I pop out onto the dance floor, right next to the DJ. Massive speakers blare music so thunderous that the vibrations make it hard to breathe. The main gym lights are turned off, but colorful lights dance on the heads of students and on the fog blowing from a machine in the corner. The air reeks of BO and too much perfume.

"Excuse me!" I call out, but my voice is lost in the noise.

I try again, screaming, only to have the same results.

How am I going to get everyone's attention if no one can hear me? My only option is to turn off those speakers. But how?

Think, Candy. Think.

I scan the DJ stand and stop on the power strip connected to the outlet. It's partially hidden by the bleachers folded up against the wall. Bingo! Speakers can't play music if they don't have a power source. Making sure no one is watching, I tiptoe to the strip.

My knees quake as I sink to the ground, hands hovering over the glowing red switch. I swallow thickly. This is it. Here goes nothing. I press the switch.

The fast-paced song stops. A collective gasp sounds in the gymnasium. Everyone turns toward the sound system, wondering what is going on.

"What are you doing!" the DJ shouts at me. "Do you know how much this equipment costs? You could have short circuited it!" He turns toward a teacher monitoring the dance and cups his hands around his mouth. "Can I get some help over here? You should really figure out how to control your students better."

I suck in a breath as the teacher locks gazes with me, glowering. He begins marching toward us. It's now or never.

I turn to the folded bleachers and climb. Voices shout, "what are you doing?" and "are you crazy?" I stop halfway to the top, high enough so the teachers can't pull me down, and face the crowd. Everyone watches me.

Phase One of my plan is complete. Now, for Phase Two.

"I, uh, hello—My name is Candy Sky," I grind out like rusted gears struggling to turn.

Judging by the incredulous looks on everyone's face, they know who I am. I gulp and wish I hadn't ditched so many public speaking classes last year. It might also have been helpful if I had written down what I wanted to say.

Sayer steps through the crowd until he's below me. He sports a blue dress shirt and black slacks. His normal cloud of hair has been braided into cornrows that lead to a fuzzy bun at the back of his head. He gives me two thumbs up with gloveless hands.

I nod. His presence lifts my confidence. If Sayer can break his curse, then so can I.

"I need to come clean about some things . . . a lot of things, actually." I tighten my sweaty grip on the metal rails. "I may have lied…about who I am—that I'm a swimming champion, a straight-A student, and a rich girl who can afford designer clothes. It's all untrue. I also don't have a famous cousin launching a morning talk show, nor am I dating Elijah Nole. My mom isn't some deadbeat party girl who drinks asparagus-peanut butter smoothies and goes days without checking on her daughter. In fact, she's the most coffee-addicted, clean-obsessed, over-protective mother in the world.

"As for my dad," I chuckle guiltily, "he's one of the most annoying, uncool people on Earth, in the Dad—kinda way. He makes me work on weekends at the Calico Oyster, and he forces me to study math printouts in his office. He pulls embarrassing pranks when I have friends over, and he belches at the most inappropriate times. He makes sure I'm fed, protected, and comforted when I'm sad." I pause, catching my breath, before I whisper to myself, "I wouldn't have my dad any other way."

I choke a little, and my eyes water. I take a breath to calm down, shoving down the urge to cry. I'll do that later. I don't have much time. Three teachers stand below me, demanding I climb down.

"Lying became a game for me, like fishing. I took pride in all the times I fooled someone into giving me what I wanted. It became a part of my identity. Who is Candy Sky without lying?" I stop and listen to the murmurs and antsy rustle of the students. A security guard appears in the doorway of the gym, and I know I will have to wrap this up. "Recently, with the help of a certain magical English teacher, I learned the things that matter most to me have nothing to do with wealth or popularity. Relationships cannot be built on the unstable base of lies. They are earned through trust and honest commitment. I hope, one day, that I'll get a second chance with the people I love."

I don't know what I expect to happen when I finally come to an end. A couple of students boo and yell that I'm holding up the dance. Almost everyone is staring as though I have three heads. With a disappointed sigh, I accept my fate and begin my descent down the folded bleachers. The security guard has joined the queue of adults waiting to chew my ears off. The principal follows, not far behind.

Looks like I'll have to come up with another plan to break the curse. At least I feel lighter with all that weight off my shoulders.

As soon as my feet hit the ground, the air electrifies. Black licorice wafts in the air. Slow clapping echoes in the painfully silent gymnasium. That's when I realize everyone is frozen in place, just like at the Calico Oyster when Mrs. Gulligan placed her curse. Only Sayer is unaffected, spinning around in shock.

Mrs. Gulligan emerges from the crowd. Her wrinkly hands are the source of the eerie clapping. Her pineapple-print dress and flamingo earrings deceive the truth about Mrs. Gulligan. She's an incredibly powerful witch.

"Congratulations on learning your lessons," Mrs. Gulligan says.

A strangled noise escapes Sayer's mouth, and he staggers in front of her. His back shakes as he blubbers, "I'm so, *so* sorry for stealing your paycheck. It was for . . . I mean, there's no excuse. I promise that I saved the money to give back to you, but the elves . . ." Sayer trails off.

"I forgive you." Mrs. Gulligan surprises both of us. "Especially now that I know about your father."

"H-How . . . ?"

"How do I know?" Mrs. Gulligan finishes for him. "I've been keeping tabs on the two of you. And it's a good thing I did." She turns to me. "I doubt you'd last another week if any more of your lies came true."

I exhale and rub my chin sheepishly. "I know, I know. I promise to never lie again."

Mrs. Gulligan tuts. "You shouldn't completely give up lying. There are times when it's necessary, such as lying that your parents are nearby when a stranger makes you uncomfortable or lying about needing to do chores when your friends are putting you in a dangerous situation. However, lying should never be used to manipulate another individual, shirk responsibilities, or evade consequences. Not only do you damage the relationships important to you, but you also hurt yourself."

I swallow and look down at my dirty socks. I understand now how it feels to be lied to. I also learned how lies can destroy others, like with Maggie. But most of all, I recognize how I put the fantasy of Elijah Nole, as well as the things I selfishly wanted, ahead of the people that I loved. I never realized what I had until I lost Mom, Dad, and Maggie.

I sniff and wipe the tears from my cheeks. I gasp when fingers catch my chin and force me to look up. Mrs. Gulligan's gaze softens, no longer the beady eye of a vulture sizing up its prey.

"Are you ready to face the consequences of your actions?" Mrs. Gulligan asks.

I nod confidently. "I am."

She smiles and steps away. The stench of black licorice intensifies until it's choking. Eyes watering, I bend over, gasping for air. Sayer places a hand on my back. He pulls his shirt over his face, trying and failing to breathe through it.

Mrs. Gulligan claps her hands twice, and she disappears.

The gym booms back to life.

NINETEEN
Home Again

Music vibrates my chest, and it takes me a moment to realize the Fall Equinox Dance continues as though nothing happened. It is like I didn't just break a ton of school rules, and Mrs. Gulligan didn't use magic to make the world stand still. The fabric of my dress shifts, growing heavier and scratchier. I look down and gasp at the pink, ruffly dress I picked out for the dance two weeks ago at a thrift shop. I'm also wearing lattice sandals, not dirty socks!

Even better, the familiar weight and jingle of my friendship bracelet is back.

"I did it," I whisper. "I broke the curse."

I notice Sayer ogling my clothes. Breath catching in my throat, I launch myself at him and squeeze him in a hug. My knees buckle in relief, and Sayer staggers under my weight. I bury my face in his shoulder and cry.

I'm finally home! No more Cursed World. I never want to go through that again.

Sayer pats my back before he peels me off of him. "I don't want anyone getting the wrong idea," he mumbles.

I sniff and step back, glaring half-heartedly. I'm too ecstatic to be offended.

"What now?" Sayer asks.

A face in the crowd catches my attention before I can respond. Behind Sayer, across the gymnasium, wearing a teal dress with floral embroidery, is Maggie. She leans her back against the wall and crosses her arms. Her foot taps the floor as though she's waiting for someone.

I swallow. My legs move on their own accord. The music, lights, and everyone in the gym melt away until it's only me and Maggie. I have to get to her. I have to touch her. I have to make sure this is real.

A hand grabs my wrist, and I break from the trance. I whip my head toward whoever is preventing me from being with my best friend.

Laurell and Elijah Nole.

They appear exactly like they had at the dance in the Cursed World. Of course, they aren't green around the gills. Too bad I don't have any more lobster shells in my purse.

"We wanna talk to you more about your cousin," Laurell offers a sickly-sweet smile. "You wouldn't want to pass up an opportunity to interview Elijah Nole, would you?"

The pop singer puffs out his chest and pretends to stare at something in the distance. He adjusts his tie all cool like. I roll my eyes.

"I lied," I say.

Laurell blinks. "What?"

"Yolanda Nox isn't real. I made her up. Now, could you excuse me?" I push past them and continue toward Maggie.

I break into a run and bounce off students in my way. Hardly anyone is actually dancing, just standing around and talking. A few couples sway in front of the DJ, but their movements are awkward, and they seem too embarrassed to look at each other.

Maggie perks up when I barrel toward her. She pushes off the wall just as I throw myself at her, and she catches me. I rock her in a bone crushing embrace.

Maggie grunts. "What's gotten into you?"

"I've missed you so much," I say, inhaling the cherry-coke scent of her lip balm.

"We came to the dance together," she says.

"We did?" I lean back to look at her face, keeping my arms loosely around her waist. "Who were you waiting for?"

"You! You needed to use the restroom. Thanks for taking forever, by the way."

"Huh." It's like I never left my world. Maybe Mrs. Gulligan made a decoy version of me?

"I don't know what is going on with you. All week, you've acted like a zombie. This is the most normal I've seen you. Did something happen?"

"You wouldn't believe me if I told you."

"I trust you."

I frown, gut squirming. I certainly don't deserve her trust after everything I've done.

"Later. I have something else I need to say." I lead Maggie to a corner, so we're out of earshot. Taking her hands in my own, I admire the natural waves of her hair, let down from her signature braid. She wears a pin with "SASS: Save Aplysia Sea Slugs" written across it on the shoulder of her dress.

"I'm sorry for always putting you in awkward situations by lying," I say. "And I'm sorry for always putting my obsession with Elijah Nole ahead of you. I don't know why you've stayed friends with me for so long, but I'm grateful for it. You're the most important person in my life, and I don't want to lose what I have with you over lies."

Maggie whistles, eyes wide with shock. I bite my lip when she doesn't say anything. Was that speech too corny? Does she think I'm joking around? Maybe I'm coming off too juvenile.

Maggie runs a hand through her hair. Her matching friendship bracelet clinks as she moves.

"Well, this is an unexpected development. I never thought I'd see the day when you apologize—let alone acknowledge your lying streak." Maggie's lips twitch slowly into a grin.

Now, it's her who attacks me, lifting me off my feet. My back pops, and I wheeze for her to put me down.

"I forgive you, because I'm awesome like that," Maggie says.

"Totally awesome," I agree.

I have my best friend back! Nothing can make this moment better . . . except hearing from my parents.

"Mom! Dad!" I cry. I almost forgot about them.

Whipping out my phone, I open a group chat and text them. *You are the lamest but greatest parents in the world!*

Mom's response is instant. *I love you, too. Is everything all right? Need me to come get you?*

I drop my head on the screen, relieved. I have my mom back! I'm free of the neglectful, lie-to-her-daughter clone in the Cursed World.

What about Dad? *I'm OK. Miss you a whole lot. Have you heard from Dad?*

I bite my lip. Although I'm no longer in the Cursed World, a part of me fears he's still missing.

Thank goodness that Mom is paying attention to her phone. *It's Saturday, so he's pretty busy. I heard from him last night.*

That's better than nothing. A thousand times better! *Do you think we can stop at the Calico Oyster after the dance?*

I can almost feel Mom's confusion. *Sure?*

"Candy?" Maggie calls.

"Sorry, sorry!" I stow my phone in my purse.

The song changes, and I remember that we're at a dance. The idea of joining dozens of sweaty bodies no longer has the same appeal as when I stole a poster for my bathroom mirror. I kinda want alone time with Maggie.

"Do you want to stay? Or do you want to go and, I don't know, see a movie or something?" I ask.

"You want to leave!" Maggie exclaims. "After we just got here! You've been dreaming about this forever!"

"Yeah, well, the dance is kinda my thing. I dragged you into it," I shrug.

Maggie thumbs one of the flowers on her dress. "First of all, I didn't get all dressed up so we can ditch. And secondly, as long as we're together, the dance is *our* thing."

Without another word, Maggie drags me to the middle of the dance floor. She winks before bobbing her head to the beat of the music.

Bending her knees, she begins bouncing up and down, stepping side to side. She raises both arms in the air and snaps her fingers.

I burst out laughing. She looks ridiculous!

Whatever. I don't care what people think of us. I copy her dance moves.

"So, are you going to tell me what's gotten into you?" Maggie shimmies before twirling on one foot. She loses balance and knocks into me, and we both snort.

"You are not going to believe me," I repeat myself. "But do you remember that rumor you told me about Mrs. Gulligan being a witch . . .?"

New Message

To : <Samantha Sky>

Subject : Candice Sky

To the Parents or Guardians of Candice Sky,

I appreciate meeting you at parent-teacher conferences after so many sabotaged attempts. I am happy to announce that your daughter has submitted all of her missing assignments. Although I cannot give her full credit for late work, she earned enough points back to bump her failing grade up to a passing one.

Candice is certainly turning a new leaf.
I look forward to her success!

Sincerely,
Mrs. Gulligan
7th & 8th Grade
English Teacher

P.S. Have you thought about signing Candice up for my Hidden Coven Writing Club? She certainly has the imagination for crafting stories. Perhaps it would provide her a healthier outlet than lying.

Send

ACKNOWLEDGEMENTS

Writing a book is a community effort. I never felt serious about finishing a draft and publishing a book until I met with other writers and joined critique groups. Through them, I gained the tools and confidence I needed to succeed. I also met a number of talented writers, who I hope will remain lifelong friends.

Brooke Adams Law, my first developmental editor, earned my first shout out. She saw the bones of this book. Brooke helped me develop three-dimensional characters and pinpoint the direction I needed to take with my story. Of course, that meant rewriting eighty percent of my book. But, in her words, "Being willing to rewrite makes you a good writer."

Halie Fewkes, my second developmental editor, honed my story into what you're reading today. Originally, CSTAL felt like two separate plots mashed together, kind of like an asparagus-peanut butter smoothie. Halie helped me cut, rearrange, and finish the ending of my book. I have learned so much from Halie, Tally Ink, and the 60 Day Novel Writing Challenge. I cannot wait to write more books with her wonderful and supportive community.

Colleen Mitchell, my book coach, guided me through the publishing process. She helped me overcome mental hurdles, procrastination, and self-doubt. I will always be grateful for the Character Decision Model she taught me, and I now use it to outline my stories.

Angelique Modin, my amazing cover artist, went above and beyond what I envisioned for the cover. She understood the style I wanted and provided exceptional suggestions when I struggled with ideas. Seeing my characters in the flesh for the first time was an incredible feeling, and it served as motivation for getting my book done.

Lauren Loftis, my copy editor, has one of the sharpest minds I have met. Along with copyediting my book, she led a critique group where I met Abbie, Beth, Christina, Christy, Elizabeth, Katie, Karilyn, and Scarlett—all of whom read excerpts of my book and provided exceptional feedback. More than writing buddies, they became friends who I will forever keep close to my heart. I'm incredibly thankful of Lauren and Tally Ink for providing a means for writers to connect.

LeighAnn Sutton, my graphic illustrator and formatter, saw my book through the final steps of publishing. She drew the coolest (and most hilarious) chapter illustrations, and she designed the interior graphics, including the emails and letters. The publishing process was daunting, but with the help of everyone from the Tally Ink team, I fulfilled my dream of becoming a published author.

Cathy Gilbert, my aunt and proofreader, endured my daily ramblings about CSTAL. I've never met someone who devours books like her, and I feel honored that she offered to proofread my book. Nothing escapes her bookworm eyes.

Brooklyn McKiernan, my tween proofreader, gave a target audience's perspective of my book. I found her feedback more nerve-wracking than my editors' and critique group's. It's readers like Brooklyn who make writing worth it.

Michelle Ellingford, my inspiration for crafting novels, had been my writing buddy since middle school. We've exchanged ideas and portions of our work for over fifteen years. She witnessed the entire development of CSTAL, from when I started the first iteration for Camp NaNoWriMo to celebrating with me on my launch day. I'm grateful for our almost-daily virtual write-ins.

Mom, my cheerleader and unofficial web content manager, instructed me on website design and marketing graphics. She set me up with the tools needed to increase traffic on my social media accounts and build a strong and positive web presence. Furthermore, she coached me on public speaking.

Sarah McKiernan and Megan Mills, my mental support team, let me blab about my book whenever I needed to and understood when I had to reschedule plans for meetings and publishing commitments. I appreciated their patience.

My husband, Gordon. I saved the best for last. He acted as my toddler distractor, plot generator, and coffee maker while I wrote CSTAL. I couldn't have published it without him.

Thank you to everyone who went through this journey with me, and thank you to the family, friends, and teachers who encouraged my writing passion. If I could give one piece of advice to an aspiring author, it would be to get others involved with your book. Writing is a long journey, and you shouldn't do it alone.

TWO TRUTHS AND ONE LIE ABOUT SHANNA P. LOWE

Shanna P. Lowe started writing when she was in preschool. She would carry around seed catalogs and copy them word for word into her notebook.

Shanna P. Lowes shares her birthday with The Land Before Time. You better believe she loves dinosaurs!

Shanna P. Lowe is completely and totally, 100% in control of her life. She knows exactly what she needs to do and where she needs to go. She certainly is not a hot mess.

FOLLOW THE AUTHOR

www.shannaplowe.com

Twitter: @ShannaPLowe

Instagram: @Author_Shanna.P.Lowe

Made in the USA
Las Vegas, NV
19 September 2022